_"It's d_

Joe asked. "Look, I just thought it would be strange if two married people didn't kiss."

Marty nodded, unable to speak.

"I figured Cody's insecure about his daddy being gone. Maybe if he feels safe, his memory will return."

And you'll be free of this burden. Marty had to remember that. Like her ex-husband, Joe didn't want a family. Responsibility to a cowboy was like a heavy saddle on a wild Mustang. They would always buck against it.

"It won't happen again," he said, with conviction. His gaze dropped to her mouth and made her insides tighten. "Unless…"

"Unless?" Her stomach rolled over. She realized she wanted him to kiss her again. She stole a glance at his wide mouth, remembering its effect on her. As quickly as they'd arisen, she stomped down those irrational thoughts. She wouldn't get involved with Joe. She wouldn't get involved with _any_ cowboy.

Ever.

Dear Reader,

You'll find the heartwarming themes of love and family in our November Romance novels. First up, longtime reader favorite Arlene James portrays *A Bride To Honor*. In this VIRGIN BRIDES title, a pretty party planner falls for a charming tycoon...whom another woman seeks to rope into a loveless marriage! But can honorable love prevail?

A little tyke takes a tumble, then awakes to ask a rough-hewn rancher, *Are You My Daddy?* So starts Leanna Wilson's poignant, emotional romance between a mom and a FABULOUS FATHER who "pretends" he's family. Karen Rose Smith finishes her enticing series DO YOU TAKE THIS STRANGER? with *Promises, Pumpkins and Prince Charming*. A wealthy bachelor lets a gun-shy single mom believe he's just a regular guy. Will their fairy-tale romance survive the truth?

FOLLOW THAT BABY, Silhouette's exciting cross-line continuity series, comes to Romance this month with *The Daddy and the Baby Doctor* by star author Kristin Morgan. An ex-soldier single dad butts heads with a beautiful pediatrician over a missing patient. Temperatures rise, pulses race—could marriage be the cure? It's said that opposites attract, and when *The Cowboy and he Debutante* cozy up on a rustic ranch...well, you'll just have to read this TWINS ON THE DOORSTEP title by Stella Bagwell to find out! A hairdresser dreams of becoming a *Lone Star Bride* when a handsome stranger passes through town. Don't miss the finale of Linda Varner's THREE WEDDINGS AND A FAMILY miniseries!

Beloved authors Lindsay Longford, Sandra Steffen, Susan Meier and Carolyn Zane return to our lineup next month, and in the new year we launch our brand-new promotion, FAMILY MATTERS. So keep coming back to Romance!

Happy Thanksgiving!

Mary-Theresa Hussey
Senior Editor, Silhouette Romance

Please address questions and book requests to:
Silhouette Reader Service
U.S.: 3010 Walden Ave., P.O. Box 1325, Buffalo, NY 14269
Canadian: P.O. Box 609, Fort Erie, Ont. L2A 5X3

ARE YOU MY DADDY?

Leanna Wilson

Silhouette
R O M A N C E™
Published by Silhouette Books
America's Publisher of Contemporary Romance

For Dorothy Anne Love, my dearest friend,
who shared a dream… What an adventure it's been!

Acknowledgments:
To my long-suffering, always enthusiastic, ever-supportive
critique group: Alyson Brown, Tammy Hilz and
Betty Seaman, for your honesty and friendship.
Here's to more champagne celebrations!
Thanks also to Dr. Kathy Weatherford and
Laurie Vanzura for their expertise.

 SILHOUETTE BOOKS

ISBN 0-373-19331-9

ARE YOU MY DADDY?

Copyright © 1998 by Leanna Ellis

This edition published by arrangement with Harlequin Books S.A.

Printed in U.S.A.

Books by Leanna Wilson

Silhouette Romance

Strong, Silent Cowboy #1179
Christmas in July #1197
Lone Star Rancher #1231
His Tomboy Bride #1305
Are You My Daddy? #1331

LEANNA WILSON

a native Texan, was born and bred in Big D, but she's a country girl at heart. More at home dreaming up stories than lesson plans, she gave up teaching to pursue writing. Once she began putting her stories on paper, it didn't take her long to publish her first Silhouette Romance novel, *Strong, Silent Cowboy*, which won the Romance Writers of America's Golden Heart Award. She's married to a strong, not-so-silent city slicker and lives in Lewisville, Texas, with their "children"—two lively shih tzus. She loves to hear from her readers. You can write to her c/o: Leanna Wilson, P.O. Box 294277, Lewisville, TX 75029-4277.

Dear Joe,

Will you be my daddy? I'll try to be good and not
<u>in-cents</u> you like I did my real dad. He went away
and left Momma and me. We need somebody big and
strong. Like you. Somebody to make us feel safe and
loved. Can you love us?

Love, Cody

Dear Cody,

That first moment I held you in my arms changed
my life forever. When you looked up at me with such
trust, I knew I couldn't disappoint you. And when
you called me "Daddy," something welled up inside
me and I knew I would do anything for you...for
your mom.

Fathers and sons don't usually get to choose each
other. But I am proud and awed that you picked me
to be your daddy. I hope I can live up to your
expectations...and to my own. I'll do everything I
can to be the best daddy. I'm sure I'll make mistakes.
But when I do, remember that I love you and your
mom more than anything. We're a family now.

Love, ~~Joe~~ Daddy

Prologue

"Your daddy can't make it to the rodeo, Cody." His momma knelt beside him in the stands that looked out over the arena, and wrapped an arm around his middle.

Her words spun around and around in his head like a top. Sudden tears burned his eyes, but he squeezed them shut, just like when he had to take yucky medicine. He sucked in a breath and felt the hot dog he'd eaten earlier lurch to his throat. He swallowed hard. He didn't want to be a baby. Not in front of all these cowboys. But he wanted to bawl like a baby now.

"But Daddy promised," he said, trying not to whine.

"I know, sweetheart." Her brown eyes looked as sad as his black Lab puppy's when they left Scout home alone.

His momma was prettier than any of his friend's mothers. She liked to smile. She made everything fun. Even eating broccoli. He didn't know why Daddy didn't want to live with them no more.

It had to be his fault.

Cody remembered Daddy's voice like an angry bark.

Don't pester me now, boy. Can't you see I'm busy here?
He'd *agarvated* him, too. Whatever that meant. But he
hadn't meant to. He'd be good. If only Daddy would come
back.

"Do you want to go home now?" Momma asked.

He couldn't leave the rodeo. Not yet. He had to show
his daddy he wasn't a baby no more. Even if Daddy wasn't
coming. Even if Daddy might not care.

Cody stuck his hands into his jeans' pockets, the way
he'd seen his daddy do often. Momma had bought him
new jeans, 'cause he was growin' so big. New boots, too.
And chaps, like a real cowboy's. Even when he knew
Momma wouldn't spend money on herself 'cause they
were pinchin' every penny, she'd bought all this stuff for
him. So he could ride like his daddy.

And he would. He couldn't leave yet.

He sucked in a breath, taking in the smell of hot dogs
and cotton candy. He liked the rodeo. He liked the cows
and horses. Most of all, he liked watching the cowboys
ride and rope. Listening to them talk made him feel as if
his daddy was standing right beside him. It eased the
squeezing tightness in his chest.

"Come on," Momma said, standing and holding out her
hand for him to take.

"No."

She lifted one eyebrow and stared down at him.

Cody rolled his bottom lip between his teeth. "Why
couldn't Daddy come?"

Her face softened. She adjusted his hat, lifting the brim
to smooth his hair back off his forehead, then she straightened the collar of his flannel shirt. "Well, he had another
rodeo. Out in west Texas."

He'd heard that excuse before and nodded. "Paid more,
huh?"

She pressed her lips into a pencil-thin line. She blinked

hard, but Cody saw the tears swell in her eyes. "Come on, sweetheart, let's go home. I have an idea." She grinned, pretending to get all excited. But Cody felt as though he'd swallowed a fat water balloon. "We'll rent *True Grit* and pop some popcorn. Feed a little to Scout. You can stay up as late as you want, since it's not a school night."

"I wanna ride," he said, squinting against the glare of the arena lights and watching the other kids gather at the far end of the chutes with real live cowboys.

"Are you sure?" Her eyebrows squinched together.

For a horrible second he thought she was going to say no. He fisted his hands. He had to do this. He had to.

His gaze shifted to the penned sheep. They looked small from up here in the stands. Some were dirty white with small black faces and others looked like Scout, except fuzzier. They didn't look mean like the bulls his dad rode. But Cody's tummy knotted up inside. What if they were?

Once, Daddy had laughed, smiling that huge smile of his, when they'd watched the sheep buckin' contest together. Cody had been too young to ride then. But he was old enough now. He was six. Almost. At least he would be in five weeks. Momma always remembered stuff like that. But Daddy didn't.

"All right," Momma said with a sigh. "If that's what you really want."

Cody released the breath he'd held.

"I'll help you," she offered.

He glanced back at the pen. None of the other kids had their mommas with them. He shook his head and crossed his arms over his chest. "Nope. I can do it by myself."

Her brown eyes turned almost black. It was the same look she'd had when he rode his two-wheeler for the first time. "Are you sure?"

He nodded and remembered his daddy's words. *You gotta act like a man, Cody. No cryin', no throwin' fits. A cowboy's tough. Suck it in and be a man.* Cody chewed on his lower lip, swallowed the fear that welled up inside him and waited for his momma to give him a good-luck kiss. She smelled like daisies, bright and sunny.

"Put your coat on, then. I don't want you catching a cold."

"Momma!" He eyed the other cowboys. None of them wore coats. If his momma had her way, he'd be bundled up like a snowman. "I'm not cold."

"You will be."

He stepped away from her then. "I'm gonna be late."

"I'll be waiting for you," she said.

All by himself, he headed down the steps toward the other kids. His heart beat loud in his ears. He rubbed the sweat off his palms and onto the back of his jeans. He thought of his daddy and the pride that would shine in his eyes when he learned Cody rode like a cowboy. Maybe then Daddy would love him...and come home.

Chapter One

A hair-raising, high-pitched squeal ripped through Joe Rawlins like a serrated knife. He tensed. With a slow, precise motion, he lowered his Stetson and angled it toward his rawhide boots. He hunched his shoulders inside his sheepskin jacket. The brisk January breeze chilled the sweat that had suddenly popped out on his brow. He tried to ignore the herd of kids stampeding past him down the ramp toward the rodeo arena. Their laughter, giggles and excitement raked across Joe's nerves.

His gaze followed them. A hitch caught in his chest at the sight of miniature cowboy hats bobbing and slipping off sweaty brows, and pointy-toed boots scurrying and skidding along the slick wooden ramp. The kids bounded into the arena. A cloud of choking dust churned around Joe. Little bodies brushed against him. Joe's gut bucked like the recoil of a shotgun. Grinding his teeth, he refused to let his thoughts travel down that dark, shady path of regret and forced himself to turn away.

Smack against his legs, a kid ran right into him. Joe

grabbed the boy by the scruff of the neck to keep him from falling backward into the dirt. "Watch out there."

Big brown eyes, full of surprise, met his.

"You okay?" Joe asked.

Slow as molasses, the kid nodded.

Joe let go of the boy's shirt and stepped out of his path. He hooked his thumb over his shoulder toward the ruckus in the arena. "If you're in the contest, you better hurry."

The kid blinked. Long, dark lashes, too long for a boy, swooped down, shadowing the pale skin beneath his eyes, then opened once more. The kid couldn't be more than four or five, Joe thought. It had been five years since....

He stuffed the bitter memory inside him and gave the little boy a quick once-over. He was a scrawny thing. With big eyes. His tooled leather belt cinched the waistband of jeans that were rolled up to his ankles. He wore polished black boots. Kids seemed as foreign to Joe as crossing the Rio Grande. And he didn't want to gain any more knowledge in that area. Not now, anyway. Not when it was too late.

Joe started to walk off, but he noticed that no one seemed interested in this lone kid. He eyed a few rangy cowboys who rolled ropes and wrapped injuries. No concerned parent came chasing after him. No one glanced his way.

The muscles in Joe's face tightened into a frown. Cursing himself for being too soft, he knelt beside the boy, his knee pressing into the rough-hewn planks. "What's your name, kid?"

"Cody...Cody Thomas." The boy stuck his hand out with more gumption than most men Joe had met.

The gesture thawed a frozen emotion inside him, one he didn't recognize or want to acknowledge. He shook the kid's chilled hand. It felt fragile, almost like a bird's delicate wing, the skin tender, soft as a baby's compared to

Joe's larger, calloused hand. And trusting. The impact hit him like an avalanche. The kid had placed his trust in him. A mistake, Joe thought.

But in that instant he made a decision. Against his will. Against his better judgment. No matter the consequences, he'd watch out for Cody until he found the boy's parents. He hoped it wouldn't take long.

"Hello, Cody Thomas, I'm Joe Rawlins."

"I know you," Cody said, awe entering his voice. "You rode out with the flag."

Joe nodded. As a favor to an old friend, he'd ridden in the opening procession. All at once, that old quiver of expectancy had rippled through his veins. The fans' applause had roared in his ears. And for one brief moment he'd longed to be back on the circuit. Then he'd remembered. Now, he wanted to get on home. Where he belonged. The rodeo, he reminded himself, had lost its glittering appeal.

He hadn't planned on playing nursemaid to a scared kid. To hurry the procedure, he asked, "Where's your dad?"

Cody ducked his head. He kicked at a clump of red clay with his boot. "I dunno."

His forlorn voice undermined Joe's determination to avoid involvement. *Tough luck, Rawlins. You're stuck with this one.*

"My mom's sittin' up there." The kid pointed into the stands, a grin splitting his face.

Shifting on his haunches, Joe squinted against the red evening glow. A dark-haired woman, with the same wide-eyed gaze as the boy, watched them. Concern knit her brow. She stood and edged toward the aisle. Joe's instincts told him she was headed his way. He couldn't blame her. A stranger talkin' to her kid. But an odd feeling surged inside him, and he stifled it with relief. He'd soon be on his way—alone.

After one last glance at the pretty brunette, and certain he didn't want to meet the lady—any lady, for that matter—he shifted back to the boy, and nudged the brim of his hat up a notch with his thumb. "Your momma's headed this way."

The boy's jaw jutted forward. "I'm gonna ride a bull."

Joe cocked a brow and suppressed a laugh.

Cody shuffled closer, hooked his hand around Joe's ear and whispered, "I ain't gonna ride a real bull. But I purrtend."

"I see. So, you're gonna get on one of those mean, surly sheep down there."

The kid nodded, excitement gleaming in his eyes.

"They can be just as tough and ornery." Joe surprised himself with a smile. "Scoot on down there before you miss your turn."

Cody took a step down the ramp, then turned back. "Will you go with me, Joe?" His face reddened, the tips of his ears turning scarlet. "I ain't never done it before."

Damn. He had to say no. He had to walk away. He didn't want anything to do with this kid, but a warm memory of his own pa teaching him to ride and rope and sit a saddle filled his mind. An ache resonated in his chest. He'd never had that privilege with his own son.

Those brown eyes stared up at him with such hope, such trust. His throat closed off the word he wanted to say. He tried to ignore the kid's effect on him, but his gut contracted like a hand fisted into a tight ball. With an irritated exhaled breath, Joe pushed against his knees and stood straight, hearing the familiar creak in his joints. "I've got other things to do, kid. Your momma can help you."

The boy's freckled features frowned. "None of the other kids are holdin' their momma's hands," he muttered, his shoulders hunching forward as he turned away. "'Bye, Joe."

Guilt inched through him as he watched the kid saunter down the ramp, his little boot heels clunking against the wooden planks. Those narrow shoulders beneath the red plaid flannel looked as if they carried the weight of the world. No kid wanted his momma—not when he needed his daddy. Where was Cody's dad? Why wasn't he here? Joe shouldn't care, dammit, but he did.

In two strides, he caught up with Cody. The kid glanced up at him and a big grin swallowed his startled expression.

"I can spare a couple of minutes," Joe said, his voice as rough as sandpaper. "But that's all."

"It won't take long." Cody slipped his hand into Joe's.

Tenderness welled inside him, but he squashed it with rock-hard determination. He shook off the kid's grip and instantly regretted his hasty action. As an unstated apology, he laid a hand along the back of the boy's neck. "Okay, how old are you?"

"Six." Cody cut his eyes toward the arena and in a softer voice added, "Almost."

"So, you're five."

The boy nodded, casting his gaze on the ground.

"Well, that's good," Joe said, giving his shoulder a gentle squeeze. "Six is too old. But five, now that's the perfect age to start riding. That's when I started."

"Really?"

Joe nodded, remembering with fondness his early years on the rodeo circuit. Then he remembered why he'd quit. "Sure is."

Together, they stepped into the arena. Their boot heels sank into the soft dirt. The announcer's booming voice echoed through the stands as he described the event for six-year-olds and under. Joe and Cody took their place at the back of the line. A mixture of applause and laughter rippled through the crowd as one by one each munchkin-size cowboy took a turn. A biting breeze nipped at Joe's cheeks. He noticed that the other kids were taller and sturdier than Cody. But in the boy's eyes, he saw all heart.

Uncomfortable with his sudden role as baby-sitter, Joe glanced at the other kids standing in line. Several waved at parents in the stands. One started bawling. Others couldn't seem to stand still, as if they had ants in their pants. Joe's nerves began to twist into knots. Kids gave him the jitters. Made him remember things....

When the kid looked up at him expectantly, Joe felt as awkward as a green colt. What should he say? Why did he have to say anything? Why didn't he say adios and be done with it?

"I wanna be a cowboy like my daddy." Cody's gaze studied Joe for a long, uncomfortable moment. "You're a cowboy." His gaze shifted to Joe's oval-shaped, silver belt buckle—his proof of worth in the rodeo arena.

A surge of pride was trampled by a stampede of guilt at the price Joe'd paid—that others had paid for him.

"You're a world champion," Cody continued. "I heard the announcer say so."

Once. Okay, three times, but certainly not anymore. The distinction held no honor. Joe hooked his thumb through his belt loop. He hadn't ridden bulls or broncs in five years. Not since— He wouldn't think of that rainy night now. He'd made his decision. Now, he was paying the price. "Not lately."

The kid's mouth pulled to one side. "My daddy rides bulls."

"He does, huh?" The kid's last name connected with another in Joe's mind. "Is your dad Flint Thomas?"

The kid beamed with enthusiastic pride. The light smattering of freckles across the bridge of his nose and cheeks stretching when he smiled. "Do you know him?"

"I've seen him ride a few times."

The cowboy was all show, Joe thought. Flint Thomas

resembled a Christmas tree, strutting in his studs and fringed rig, with pretty girls hanging on his arms like ornaments. The last time Joe'd seen him ride, Flint had landed on his arrogant butt. That hadn't stopped the belt buckle bunnies from chasing after him. Once again, Joe eyed Cody's momma, the dark-haired woman who'd moved to the rails surrounding the arena. She was a looker, a damn sight for sore eyes. And he'd best keep his off her. He wondered why Flint bothered with other women. Shrugging off his odd notion, he figured it wasn't his business or concern. Neither was this kid.

Cody had his own daddy. He didn't need Joe. But Flint was out doing what Joe had once done—sacrificing time with family for one chance at immortality—trying to be the best cowboy in the world. Joe had succeeded. Or had he? He'd won that damn title. But what had he lost? Had the price been too high? In the end, the title meant nothing, nothing without his wife or—

The boy tugged on the edge of his sleeve. "What do I do, Joe?"

The kid's plea stopped him from charging out of the arena like a rank bull. He forced himself to kneel beside Cody and brace his forearm across his knee. "There's nothing to this. That cowboy up front will set you on the back of the sheep—" Remembering the kid's pretend game, he corrected himself. "Er, bull."

Cody gave a broad smile and wink that warmed Joe from the inside out. "I don't got any spurs. Momma couldn't buy 'em."

"You won't need them. The animal won't like you sitting on his back. And he'll take off running." He adjusted the kid's chaps around his narrow hips. "Here, put on your gloves. You're gonna hold on to the rope real tight. Soon as they let that sh— bull go, he'll go to bucking. So, hang on for the ride. Okay?"

The kid nodded, his eyes even wider, if that were possible.

"You worried, cowboy?" Joe asked.

Shaking his head, the boy swallowed hard, gulping down any fear. "What if I fall?"

Joe heard the slight tremor in the last word and remembered facing his own fears. "Every cowboy falls. When you do, stand up and dust yourself off."

"Have you ever fallen?"

"More than my share." He tugged on the brim of the little boy's hat. "You'll be fine."

Together, they watched the boy in front of them bobble on the back of a sheep and topple to the ground in less than a second. Stunned, the red-haired boy was lifted onto his feet by a burly cowboy and handed his hat. "Next."

Joe clapped Cody on the back. "Let's give it a go."

Following the directions from the lead cowboy, Joe lifted Cody onto the back of a fluffy black-faced sheep. Another cowboy held the animal with a rope hooked to its halter. The kid stuck his gloved hand through the looped rope. His face squinched up into a mask of concentration.

"I'm ready," Cody said, his pip-squeaking voice making Joe want to step forward and call a halt to this charade.

A cowboy gave a whoop and released the animal. Joe held his breath and watched. The sheep bounded forward, jostling Cody. But he held fast. His jaw jutted forward with determination. His hat slid backward. Seconds ticked by, but he held on. He took a bounce and slid off his perch toward the animal's rump. The rope flew out of his grasp, and he flipped backward to the ground. He landed sprawled facedown in the dirt.

A grin sprang to Joe's lips. Cody had done a fine job. He started to clap, but the quiet stillness of the little boy's body made his blood freeze solid in his veins. A band of fear gripped his chest.

An unearthly silence descended on the arena. The echo of his own heartbeat filled Joe's ears with a roar. He took three running steps and slid on his knees to Cody's side.

"Don't move him," he shouted to no one in particular. He was the first to reach the kid, but several other cowboys closed in fast. Laying a gentle hand on the boy's back, Joe felt a steady heartbeat and the slow rise and fall of his rib cage with each breath. He leaned down and peered at the frozen little features, chalky white skin accented by those long, swooping lashes.

"Cody? Son?" The word slipped accidentally through his stiff lips. "You okay?"

Faint movement beneath the lightly veined eyelids gave Joe hope, then the kid's eyes fluttered open. He looked dazed. It took a moment for his gaze to focus on Joe. His pale lips moved. Joe edged closer, straining his ears. "What was that, son?"

"Daddy."

The word sliced through Joe's defenses and plunged a dagger in his heart.

"He'll be fine," the rodeo doctor said, eyeing the blossoming bruise on Cody's forehead.

Marty Thomas swallowed back a rush of tears. Now wasn't the time. Stay calm, she coached herself. For Cody. Only her knees didn't obey. A weakness had settled in them and she thought she might crumple to the floor. To steady herself, she sat next to her son on the examination table and gave him a smile to cover her alarm at the bulge on his forehead growing to the size of a Grade-A egg.

Her mind swam as fear loosened its grip on her. She'd held back, wary and watchful as Cody rode in the Mutton Bustin' Contest. The second she'd seen Cody lying face-down, unmoving, she'd raced into the arena, cursing herself for not saying no. Tears scalded the backs of her eyes at the terrifying memory.

She cursed her ex-husband, too. Flint had planted the seed in Cody's mind to be a cowboy, like him. It had fed his overinflated ego. She no longer cared if Flint hurt himself riding bulls and broncs, but when he endangered her son, she had to put her foot down. The anger churning inside her at the thought of her ex threaded her shredded nerves into tightly woven determination.

She skimmed her hands down the creased edges of her jeans. Earlier, fear had numbed her, but now the paralysis had given way to a shuddering chill, as cold and lonely as a wintry wind. She resented the utter helplessness she felt.

Why had she picked such a lousy husband? What would it be like to have a dependable man, one she could lean on, one she could turn to in the midst of trouble, an anchor, a support? Did someone like that even exist? No one could make problems vanish into thin air, but someone strong and capable might lighten the burden…or share it. At least the fantasy made her think so at the moment.

"I recommend Cody get a couple of X rays," the doctor continued, his thick accent like a balm to her nerves, "just to be on the safe side. It's a good sign, though, that bump on his forehead. Ugly as it is, it means it's swelling out. Not internally."

She tried to focus on the doctor's words, but they jumbled together. She smoothed a thumb over Cody's cheek, rubbing off a patch of dirt. His usually light freckles stood out dark against his pale skin. "Yes, okay, we'll see a doctor right away. He doesn't need an ambulance?"

"Nah. Get a friend to drive you over. It's not far."

A friend? She didn't know anyone here. Not anymore. Feeling the doctor's gaze settle on her, she stared at the silver tips of her boots. Boots she hadn't worn in more than two years. Not since she'd stopped coming to rodeos.

Not since her marriage had unraveled. Coming tonight had proven to be one more in a long line of mistakes.

"I can drive him myself." She hooked the strap of her purse over her shoulder and grabbed her keys.

The doctor opened his mouth, but another voice interrupted.

"I'll give you a lift."

The deep, resonating voice, full of authority, made her turn. A cowboy stood a few feet away on the other side of the medical trailer, leaning against a dark counter, his arms crossed over his wide, sturdy chest. Was this her knight in shining armor, ready to slash through her problems as easily as an army storming a castle? No, he was just a cowboy. A good-looking cowboy to boot! And that meant trouble.

A black Stetson hat sat on his head at a jaunty angle, shading his features. When he stepped forward, out of the shadows, he looked vaguely familiar. His blue eyes, bright as lasers and just as sharp, captured her attention. His keen perusal made her skin tighten and her nerves tense defensively. She recognized him as the man who'd walked into the arena with Cody.

Before she could speak, her son reached for the man, his hand opening and shutting as it once had when he'd been a baby wanting more food. "Daddy!"

Marty patted her son's shoulder. "No, Cody, your daddy's not here."

The man's square jaw flexed. His eyes narrowed on her son. She caught a glint of steel in the blue depths. A cold shiver rippled through her. Without hesitation, he crossed the room, his boot heels making a hollow sound against the tiled floor. His broad shoulder brushed hers as he moved toward her son. Irritation bucked inside her. But she didn't know if her aggravation stemmed from him or her reaction to him. Hadn't she learned about good-looking cowboys with Flint?

"If it isn't Joe Rawlins," the doctor said.

His name tugged at Marty's memory. She'd probably heard Flint mention him—another cowboy with a successful notch or two on his belt and a long line of broken hearts behind him. Her back stiffened. No cowboy would ever be her champion.

"It's been too long." The doctor held out his hand.

"Hello, Doc," Joe Rawlins said with a slow grin and firm handshake. "Are you taking good care of this kid?" His voice reminded her of sandpaper scraping across a pine board.

"Of course. He yours?" Doc asked, peering over the rim of his half glasses.

Joe gave a slight shake of his head then turned to look at the boy. He thumbed the brim of his hat and gave a brief, heart-warming smile to Cody.

She remembered the tall cowboy standing next to her son, his one hand loosely resting along Cody's smaller shoulders as the two stood with thumbs hooked in their beltloops. Like matched bookends. Her concern had escalated, but before she'd reached them they'd entered the arena. She'd forced herself to hold back, knowing Cody didn't want her coddling him. God, she'd wanted to. After all, he was her baby. But watching him, his gaze trained on this tall, handsome cowboy, she'd realized he wasn't her baby any longer. He was growing up. And he needed a male role model. But a cowboy? Please, God, no!

Resentment stirred up self-righteous anger. Cody's real father should have been standing next to their son, helping him, encouraging him, teaching him. Not some stranger. But Flint had forgotten the promise he'd made. He'd changed his mind and gone to Amarillo for a higher paying rodeo where he'd drawn a better bull.

She'd wanted to snatch her son out of the contest, but Cody had begged to try. His father had already disappointed him. How could she? She'd promised. And unlike Flint, she lived up to her promises. Now, she regretted she'd ever agreed.

"How are you doing, cowboy?" Joe asked, his drawl smooth, his tone light.

"I fell," Cody answered, his voice full of despair.

"Sure did. Best fall of the night. Why, folks'll be talking for weeks about your bravery, what a tumble you took."

Her son's eyes brightened and Marty's heart tripped over itself. "Really?" Cody asked.

Joe nodded.

"My head hurts real bad." A whine entered his voice, and concern rippled through Marty.

"It should," Joe said. "But you're gonna be okay."

Tired of the cowboy's intrusion, Marty smoothed a hand along her son's arm and drew his attention. "Think you can sit up?"

With barely a shake of his head, Cody's eyes filled with tears. "My tummy feels yucky."

"That's normal," the doctor said to Marty. "He's probably got a mild concussion. Watch if he starts vomiting. Might be a good idea for Joe to drive you to the hospital. You can trust him."

Joe nodded. "I'll drive. You watch after Cody."

"But…"

He cocked one brow at the start of her protest. His blue gaze swept over her from head to toe, and a warmth flooded her cold body.

She eyed him warily. A million questions rifled through her mind. One truth silenced them: this cowboy had helped her son, befriended him, when Cody's father hadn't even shown up. She didn't want to rely on this man. Or anyone. But for her son's sake, she would. This once.

Without asking her permission, Joe Rawlins swooped Cody up into his arms. "Come on, my truck's not far." Over his shoulder, he said, "Thanks, Doc."

"Hey!" Marty called, grabbing their coats and her purse, then running to catch up with him. "What do you think you're doing?"

"I'm taking him to the hospital." His voice had a stern edge.

"Look, Mister—" she made a grab for her glove, which fell to the ground "—I don't know who you are, but—"

"Momma!" Her son wailed. His little hand touched his head.

"What is it, Cody? Momma's here."

His arm snaked up and around the cowboy's muscular shoulder, making him appear even larger and stronger than before. Cody looked even paler against the man's stark white shirt and sheepskin jacket. "Don't yell at Daddy."

"Daddy?" Her gaze flew to meet Joe's equally startled one. "Why does he think you're his father?"

His lips thinned. "I don't know." He nodded toward a battered, faded red pickup. "Get in. We're goin' to the hospital."

This time, Marty didn't question. Her son's cries and his odd behavior frightened her. She climbed into the cab of the pickup. The cowboy tenderly laid her son across her lap, and she cradled Cody against her shoulder, shushing him, telling him it would be all right.

Eyeing the cowboy with speculation, she prayed it would. "You can drop us off at the hospital. You don't have to stay."

But he did. Joe couldn't force himself to leave.

He paced. Every few seconds he glanced at his watch, then at the double doors where Marty Thomas and her little boy had disappeared into the hustle and bustle of the emergency room. He'd tried to settle into one of the plastic-covered chairs, but he couldn't sit without shifting constantly, unable to relax. A burning antiseptic odor drove him temporarily outside to breathe in the fresher air, stare at the moon, ask himself more unanswerable questions. The jingle of keys in his pocket reminded him he could leave. Just walk away. It wasn't his responsibility. But for some reason, he always returned to the sterile waiting room.

The grating sounds of the game show on the television set perched high on a shelf added to his unease. He turned off the sound, and none of the others waiting patiently or otherwise dared confront him about it. Some read magazines. Others stared blankly at the game show and tried to read the contestant's lips. Joe paced.

He remembered Cody's cries, his mother's soothing voice. Her chocolate brown eyes filled with fear, resentment and anger. The disagreeable emotions had sprung up inside of him, too. In spite of the uncertain, distrustful glances she'd shot his way, she'd cooed and comforted her son with the gentleness only a mother could provide. Unfamiliar emotions had clogged Joe's throat and he'd kept his eyes on the road. But he couldn't block out the kid's whimpers, the mother's lilting voice.

And he'd remembered…too much.

He stuffed his hands into his front pockets and hunched his shoulders against the cold memories.

The squeak of the double doors caught his attention, and he turned on his heel. Marty Thomas swept through the opening, her gaze darting. She veered toward a bank of pay phones. Juggling her leather purse, she searched for something inside. Her frame was small, petite, like Cody's. Her black jeans and snug T-shirt accentuated her tiny waist, narrow hips and long legs.

Joe followed after her and held a coin between his fingers. "Need a quarter?"

Startled, she faced him, clutching her purse against her chest. "You're still here."

He couldn't tell from her wide-eyed expression if she was glad, irritated, or simply surprised.

Her shoulders squared as she pulled a coin out of her purse. "No, thanks. I've got one."

He shrugged and figured she wished he'd gone on home. But how could he? Doffing his hat, twirling it around in his hands, he asked the question burdening him. "How's Cody?"

"He'll be fine. After a couple of days' rest." She stuck the quarter in the coin slot.

"Did he get a concussion?" he asked.

"A mild one." She punched in a few numbers and held the receiver to her ear. After a minute of suppressed silence, she slammed the receiver into its cradle.

"Not home?" he asked.

She turned and flipped her hair off her shoulder, "Look, I appreciate your help. I do. You were...sweet to Cody." Her voice softened, as if she'd gained control of her turbulent emotions. "For that, I'm grateful. But you don't have to feel obligated to stay any longer."

"Are they keeping him here overnight?"

"No. I can take him home."

He rubbed his jaw with his thumb, the nail scratching the stubble. "Then let's go."

She stared at him, her jaw slack. "Why are you doing this?" she asked. "I mean, you don't know me. You don't know my son. Why do you want to help?"

He didn't know the answer. And he wasn't sure he wanted to find it. All he did know was that he couldn't walk away. Not yet. "I know your husband, Flint."

Her jaw hardened. Her eyes narrowed with suspicion. "Ex-husband."

Her statement surprised him. He hadn't heard the scuttlebutt that usually went with breakups in the small family of rodeo. But then he didn't run in those circles anymore. Still, based on Flint's usual indiscrete escapades, Joe couldn't say he blamed the lady for her wariness of cowboys. He'd mistakenly aligned himself with Flint. And that was a false impression.

Marty crossed her arms over her chest. "So, this is all due to the infamous cowboy code?"

"Nope. Don't know that I'd do much of anything for your *ex*-husband."

A wisp of a smile flitted across her full lips. That tiny glimpse of the softer, gentler woman unnerved him more than the thought of facing an angry, snorting bull.

She chuckled. "You must know him, all right." Releasing her arms, she crammed her hands into her pockets and ducked her head. "I appreciate your help this evening, Joe. Really, I do. But I don't want to impose. I'll call a friend to come get us."

"It's no imposition. I'm here. No use wakin' somebody out of a sound sleep." He read the hesitancy in her eyes. How could he blame her? He was a virtual stranger. She'd already taken a chance just getting in his truck for the ride to the hospital. But now he was offering a whole other proposition to take her and her son home. He wanted to relieve her concerns. "I'm not after anything."

"Then why?" Her brows slanted downward.

"I feel responsible," he confessed. The words tumbled over themselves getting out. "I put him up on that damn animal. I let him fall. I should have been there...quicker. Maybe I could have..."

I should have been there.

The words looped around his mind and dragged up the

memories he thought he'd buried. How many times had he tortured himself with those simple words? His chest tightened, squeezing his lungs until he couldn't draw even a thin breath. He should have been there five years ago. He should have been there.

That old familiar pain burned once more inside his chest. The embers had never died. Ashes covered his soul with guilt. Little reminders set off sparks that raged into a blaze of accusations and choking, smoky memories.

Guilt squeezed his heart. He blinked and swallowed hard. It was too late. Too damn late for him to redeem himself. Is that what he was trying to do here? It made no sense. He couldn't explain it to himself, much less to the woman standing in front of him.

Marty watched his expression shift and change. Closing, as if locking away his emotions. His words confused her. Why, she wondered, should he have been there? He was *there*. Faster than anyone else. Why would this stranger feel responsible when Flint acted more like a distant cousin than a father?

It was her fault, anyway. She'd given her permission for her son to ride. Maybe that explained her emotional roller coaster ride. She blamed herself for Cody's accident, even more than Flint. But Joe's statement—*I feel responsible*—set her on her heels and made her take a hard look at him. Maybe he was more…much more than she'd first thought. Which was not in the least settling.

Of course, she'd finally put two and two together. Joe Rawlins. She should have recognized him instantly. He was almost a legend around rodeo circles, having won three world championships in bull and bronc riding. He was the quintessential cowboy. Maybe that's why he irritated her so.

Why? she'd asked. Shaking his head, he said, "Hell, I don't know, lady. I'm here. Your son's a good kid. I thought I might help. It's as simple as that. I thought folks looked out for one another. I guess I thought wrong.'' He slapped his hat onto his head. ''You want me to leave. Fine. I'm out of here.''

Marty watched the proud cowboy walk away, his sheep-skin jacket tucked beneath his arm. Shame swept over her for the way she'd treated him. She should have at least thanked him. He'd given them a ride. He'd offered to help. When was the last time anyone had offered her anything, even a hand? His words sunk into her heart, burying her pride for a moment.

''Mr. Rawlins,'' she called. Her voice sounded hoarse. She cleared it and tried again. ''Joe?''

He stopped and looked back at her. He had startling blue eyes that looked right through the barriers she'd erected. Could he see she wasn't as tough as she wanted to be? Could he see her trembling, the aftereffects of fear for her son and guilt for not resisting Cody's pleas to ride a damn sheep?

Motionless, he watched her. Waited, as patient as a hunter.

Sucking in a steadying breath, she caught up to him, uncertain of what she would say, but knowing she couldn't let him leave. Not like this.

''I'm sorry.'' A quiver started in her belly and spread to her knees. She felt weak all over. ''I was ungrateful.'' She wrapped her arms around herself, holding in the emotions that shook her to the core. ''I...was wrong. I was just so worried about Cody. I've never seen him hurt like that. If anything ever happened to him—'' Her voice broke. She clamped her lips shut and fought back the urge to let loose with a good cry. Not now. There would be time for that later—when she was alone.

Joe shifted from foot to foot. When she glanced at him again, he held his hat in his hands, his fingers curling over the brim, tightening on the felt. The hat band had creased his hair. The fluorescent lights caught golden glitters shining in the thick, light brown waves. She had a sudden urge to smooth back his hair and soothe his wrinkled brow.

But he reached out to her first. Awkwardly, he yanked his hand back before he touched her. "It's okay," he said, his voice deep and rich. "I pushed too hard."

"No, you were just trying to be nice."

He nodded. "My offer still stands. I'll give you and Cody a ride home. You don't have to be afraid of me. I'm not a criminal. I'm just a cowboy trying to help."

Just a cowboy. That in itself should have warned her. But she knew her options were limited. Her first priority was Cody. "We'd appreciate that."

"I'll pull the truck around to the drive here," he said, stepping away.

Without thinking of the consequences of her actions, she stopped him with a hand on his arm. His muscles flexed beneath his starched shirt. She felt the sinews and tendons, strong and powerful, making her feel too vulnerable next to him. His strength, his warmth, weakened her resolve to stand on her own two feet. She wanted to lean into him, let him be strong for her as she'd always wished Flint had been. But she resisted the temptation. She didn't want to be disappointed again.

Pulling her hand back, she said, "I think you should know something first."

He nodded for her to continue.

"My son— Cody…well, he thinks you're his father." There, she'd said it. As weird as it seemed, she wanted Joe Rawlins to be aware of the situation. Confusion and sorrow fought for control of her emotions. It sharpened the guilt she felt over the divorce she and Flint had inflicted on poor little Cody.

Blood drained out of Joe's face. His features looked razor-sharp, the angles cutting, the jaw blunt. Grim brackets surrounded his mouth.

"You see," she went on to explain, "he has a mild form of amnesia. Nothing serious. Or so the doctor says. He seems to remember everything else. His name. That we were at the Stockyards Rodeo. Even his teacher's name. But he's forgotten that I'm divorced. And that his daddy is...somewhere else."

"Why would he think I'm his dad?" Joe asked, his voice thick.

"I'm not sure. Cody's had a rough time accepting his father's absence. Flint left—"

She resisted telling this practical stranger of the disappointment and frustration surrounding her failed marriage. She'd gotten over Flint. But obviously Cody hadn't.

"Flint's pursuing rodeo full-time now." Not that it had ever been anything different. "He doesn't come back to Fort Worth much. Even to see Cody." Though Flint had weekend visitation rights. She gripped her forearms, steadying herself. "He was supposed to be here tonight. To help Cody ride in that blasted contest. But he got a better offer, I guess."

Joe nodded. "And I befriended your son."

"That could explain it. But your kindness backfired. He thinks you're his daddy. The doctor says he should recover the missing pieces of his memory soon. But it may take a few days. He said we should humor him." She shrugged. "I don't know about that. I think I should just tell him the truth. If you don't want to get involved, that's okay. He'll be fine. You're welcome to back out now. I can call someone to pick us up."

Marty wasn't sure which she hoped for more. If he left, then she'd be on her own again. That was okay. She was used to it. But if he stayed, it might be more than she bargained for.

"What do you say?" she asked, pushing him for an answer.

"I'll give you a ride back to your car and see you get home safe. But that's all I can offer."

She nodded, appreciating his honesty. At least he didn't promise more than he could deliver. "I won't ask for anything more."

Chapter Two

Marty had a light touch. Joe watched her press a cool cloth to her son's forehead. Her hands were small and petite, like the rest of her, yet her long, delicate fingers were competent and strong at the same time. Seeing her care for her son churned up something inside Joe, something he couldn't label, something he wasn't sure he wanted to acknowledge. But it was there, inside him, twisting around his heart with each pulse, tightening, squeezing, contracting.

Joe leaned against the doorjamb in the doorway to Cody's bedroom. The wooden trim dug into his shoulder. Pulling up a pine rocker beside Cody's trundle bed, Marty sat on the edge and leaned toward her son. She smoothed the red-and-blue striped comforter over him and tucked the sheets beneath his chin. A lanky black Lab lay at the end of the bed, curled into a ball, his tail thumping against the footboard. A splash of yellow from a Snoopy night-light washed over the intimate scene of mother and son. Her skin looked like pale moonlight against the sable pelt of sleek black hair falling softly to her shoulders.

Exhaustion had settled into her features, making them taut, but she still managed a smile for her son. Her lips curved gently at the corner, pulling her mouth to the side, crinkling her cheek. Her tender half smile captivated Joe. A warm glow spread through him to diffuse the tightness in his chest. He wondered what it would be like for someone to smile like that at him. It had been so long since anyone had. He doubted he'd be around long enough for Marty to give him one of hers. She seemed to reserve her smiles for those she loved—her son. He didn't deserve her smile. Or anyone else's.

His head began to pound. He wanted to block out the pictures swirling in his head. But how could he? How could he forget his wife, his unborn child? How could he not think about what might have been?

I should have been there.

"I think we're fine now." Marty's words shattered his private thoughts with a voice as soft as a lullaby.

Mentally, he shook himself back to the present and nodded. That was his cue. Time to go. Strange how he resisted what he knew was right. His limbs felt too stiff to move, to walk out the door and out of their lives.

Clearing the lump from his throat, he coughed. "Okay. Good."

Her smile faltered. She glanced down at her sleeping son, her long lashes, so like Cody's, making the smudges beneath her eyes darker. Her hand, gentle yet possessive, settled on Cody's shoulder, her fingers plucking at the sheet. "You shouldn't feel obligated to stay, Joe. We'll be fine. You've done enough."

But had he? Had he really?

He cursed himself for mixing his fatal mistake together with this accident. One had nothing to do with the other. But why couldn't he walk out the door, leave this mother and son alone, go back to his ranch by himself? As he should.

"Momma?" Cody stirred, his legs shifting beneath the covers, rustling the sheets.

"Shh." She pressed a finger to his lips. "It's all right. Go back to sleep. I'll be right back." She kissed his forehead, her long dark hair veiling her face until she straightened.

She hooked a lock behind her small, shell-shaped ear. It gave Joe a clear shot of her long, sloping neck. Shadows played along her pale skin. He watched the way she moved, gracefully, as if she floated across the room. She glanced over her shoulder at her son and told the dog to stay with Cody. Joe felt a jerking tug on his own heart. Did she cling to her son, as he'd clung desperately to his wife's hand in those last days? He'd prayed for another chance. But those prayers had fallen on deaf ears.

"I better be going," he said, his voice gruff.

Across the room, Marty had looked confident and capable. But standing next to him, peering up at him, she seemed infinitely more vulnerable. And, dammit, he felt protective toward her. When he had no right, no cause.

He stepped away from her, away from any obligations or responsibility, and into the darkened hallway. They moved together toward the den, their footsteps muffled by the thick carpet, their clothes rustling in the still quiet of the house. Her scent, as light and delicate as her touch, reached out to him like a whisper, an invitation.

He resisted the urge to breathe in that scent, memorize it, take the blend of musk and lilies inside and hold it there. Stunned by his reaction, his senses sharpening on her, he paused for her to pass through the arched entryway into the den. With deliberate intent, he stuffed his hands into his back pockets. He'd overstayed his welcome. He had to leave. Women, he kept at arm's length. Like kids. He never wanted to disappoint one again. He never wanted to fail as he had with Samantha and his baby.

"I appreciate all of your help," Marty said, her voice heavy, hoarse. "Really, I do. I didn't mean for it to take this long. It was kind of you to help us."

"My pleasure," he said. "If there's anything else I can do..." He let the words hang between them like intimate apparel on a clothesline, flapping in the soft breeze. *Don't promise anything!* He warned himself to get the heck out of her house. Fast. *Before you hurt someone else.*

"Daddy?" Cody's cry stopped Marty from opening the door and Joe from leaving.

A crease pinched her brow. His gut contracted. His ears burned with the sound of that word as it sunk deep into his soul. Immediately, Marty retraced her steps. Behind her, she stretched out her hand, giving Joe a silent message to stay back, to make his escape. While he could. She could handle the situation. Cody was her son. Not his.

But he couldn't. For some insane reason, he couldn't turn his back on her or Cody. After all, he'd called for Joe. *No, he called for his daddy. That's not you.* But at the moment the young boy thought Joe was his daddy. How could he disappoint him? How could he run like a coward?

"Daddy!" Cody called again, his voice taking on a higher pitch and deciding Joe's fate.

Cursing himself, he caught up with Marty and brushed past her. He entered her son's room. The dog sat up on the end of the bed, his watchful eyes shifting from Joe to Cody. "I, uh...hey, cowboy."

"Where are you going?" Those wide, expressive eyes stared up at him, blinking back fear.

Joe ignored the question and knelt beside the bed. He removed his hat and placed it on top of the little boy's tummy. "You're looking better. How are you feeling?"

His hand inched out from under the covers and finger-walked across his brow. "My head hurts."

"I bet it does. But you're gonna be just fine."

"Are you going somewhere?" Cody asked.

"Well, I, uh…" Joe stumbled over an excuse, not sure what to tell this teary-eyed kid.

Marty hovered at the end of the bed, her fingers curled around Scout's collar. "Cody, honey, it's all right. Joe, um, I mean your—"

"Your momma's here to watch over you, cowboy."

"But I want *you.*" Cody's bottom lip rolled outward.

Joe's gut twisted into a corkscrew of doubt. What now? Should he just tell the kid flat-out that he wasn't his daddy, never would be? The muscles along his neck pinched his nerves. No, he couldn't do that. He couldn't deliberately hurt the little boy.

"Well, sure, cowboy, and I want to stay. But…" His gaze sought Marty's. He read fear, uncertainty in those dark depths. He walked a tightrope, not wanting to upset Cody and not wanting to defy his mother's wishes. But what was he supposed to do?

A vulnerable glimmer in her eyes made him think she wanted him to stay. However, her body language—the stern jaw and one fisted hand propped on her hip—gave him a whole different message. "I've got another rodeo," he said, avoiding the kid's direct stare. "Tomorrow."

"Where?" A frown puckered his little brow.

"Oklahoma." He stuck his hat onto his head, cursing himself for lying.

"Can I come?" A hopeful lilt entered Cody's voice.

"Not this time." He tried a careless smile and chucked the boy gently on the chin. "I can't handle the competition. You're too tough for me."

A faint smile flickered across the boy's lips. "Will you come back after that?"

He didn't dare look at Marty. He knew she'd want him
to refuse. But how could he? Maybe by Monday the kid
would have forgotten all of this nonsense. Maybe by then
he'd have forgotten Joe existed. But Joe would never forget this little boy who'd called him daddy. And his feisty,
brown-eyed mother.

"Yeah, of course," he agreed. He felt Marty's gaze like
daggers in his back. He brushed aside a lock of hair off
the kid's forehead. The sight of his dark, protruding bruise
reminded Joe why he owed something to this kid and his
mom. "You be good for your momma until then, okay?"

Cody nodded, his hair brushing against the fluffy pillow.
"When will you be home, Daddy?"

Something inside Joe burned, the sparks flaring into a
blaze. He felt himself disintegrating, falling apart, being
consumed by the need to hear that again.

Daddy.

But that wasn't him. He swallowed hard. "Soon, son,
soon."

"What do you mean, *soon?*" Marty braced her hands
on her hips and glared at the cowboy. He stood with his
hat in his hands, his gaze on his boots. She'd all but pushed
him out of her son's room, down the hall and closed the
door to the hallway so they could have a private conversation without the benefit of five-year-old ears. How dare
he promise her son he'd return! How dare he set her son
up for another disappointment!

"What was I supposed to say?" Joe countered, his voice
rough. He rolled his hat over and over. His gaze lifted and
locked with hers. Crystal-blue sparks ignited with a flash
of defensiveness. "Did you want me to tell Cody, 'No,
son, I'm never coming back.' Would that have satisfied
you?"

Her mouth twisted. He'd yanked the plug out of her

anger. She dragged her fingers through her long hair. What was the right answer? Should they lie? Or dash a young boy's hopes in one fell swoop? Which would hurt Cody more?

She imagined her son's disappointment when Joe never showed up again. Cowboys, after all, rarely did. They lived a rambling life, on their own terms, without regard for how they treated others. Of course, if someone was as cruel to an animal and treated it with as little respect, a cowboy would throttle the abuser. But family played second fiddle to work and rodeo. Hadn't she learned that the hard way? Her anger returned as she pictured her son watching and waiting for Joe, as he'd waited so many times for Flint.

"What were you doing?" she asked. "Trying to confuse him?"

"No. I thought you wanted me to play along." Joe balanced his Stetson between his hands.

"Where did you get that idea?"

"From what you said at the hospital. The doctor wanted to keep him calm, provide a safe environment for his memory to return. Humor him, remember? Wouldn't that mean be a father to him? Rather than desert him?"

"You're *not* his father."

A glimmer of pain flashed in his blue eyes.

Marty brushed aside the incessant tapping on her conscience. She owed this man nothing. Her only responsibility belonged with her son. "There's a difference in making him feel secure and telling him a blatant lie."

"I didn't lie." His ears reddened. "Not about that. I gave an excuse for why I was leaving."

Her heartbeat quickened at the prospect. For some reason, one she couldn't fathom, she wanted to believe Joe was different from her ex. She wanted to believe he would come back. That he had good intentions. That he was dependable. That he had a kind, tender heart. She wanted to believe, hope, trust. Again. In fact, he'd forced her into that position. It unraveled her nerves.

She crossed her arms over her chest as much to protect herself as to hold off the cold dread seeping into her bones. "So, you are planning to come back?"

"I guess I will."

"You guess!" Her wire-thin patience snapped. In her mind, she saw Cody's hopes, once again, crushed. "Is that yes or no? Will this just be a later disappointment? When you don't show up?"

His jaw clenched, his mouth thinning into a tight line of determination. "No."

"You called him 'son,' for God's sake." A tremor began deep inside her. She felt the weight of responsibility crushing her. "You *promised* you'd come back."

Silence followed her brief explosion. Guilt settled around her heart like scattered debris. What had gotten into her? She was usually calm, in control. But fear sapped her strength. She was fighting—herself, her anger—for every ounce of control. Her limbs trembled. She realized she was punishing Joe for Flint's mistakes. Her gaze met his, curious and wary of this man at the same time. Regret tempered her voice. "Why did you call him 'son'?"

Joe pinched the bridge of his nose, squeezing his eyes shut for a long moment. "I didn't know I had until just now." He shrugged, his broad shoulders lifting, straining the seams of his white button-down as if it had suddenly shrunk. "He looked up at me with those big brown eyes, pleading. I... Hell. I don't know."

She saw a split second of pain deepen his eyes to a midnight-blue. As rapid as a blink, an icy cold froze them once more. Somehow they caused a flash of warmth inside her. Her response disturbed her. She chafed her arms, trying to remove the unnerving tingling inside her.

"It's neither here nor there," she said, doubting Joe

would ever come back. Flint sure hadn't. Why would this cowboy be any different? "I'll fix the damage you've caused."

His features hardened like stone. For a long moment he stared at her, his gaze dull and lifeless. Then something snapped. His eyes glittered like bits and pieces of gems, the light catching on the sharper edges. "What the hell do you want, lady?" He slapped his hat onto his head. "I gave you my word. That's all I have. Whether you like it or not, I'm coming back. Not because I want to. Not because of you, either. I'm coming back because I made a promise to your boy in there."

His flat tone, his stern expression, felt like a physical blow. Her legs began to quake. Fatigue collapsed on top of her. Her heart contracted with guilt. The tight control she held on her emotions loosened another notch.

He turned and stalked to the door. Just like Flint. But Joe had no responsibilities here. None at all. Yet his words, full of conviction, rang in her ears, echoed in her heart. He owed her nothing. She owed him her gratitude. After all, this man had wasted his evening driving her and Cody to and from the hospital. She owed him thanks, not derision. He hadn't asked for her son to call him daddy. He hadn't asked for any of it.

"Wait. Joe, please." She caught the door with her hand before he slammed it closed. The cold night air slapped against her face.

Joe kept walking, his boot heels cursing her with each thwack against the concrete walk. His shoulders squared, his back stiffening against her plea.

A chill arced through her. He was leaving...leaving her, as her ex had so often done. Usually she didn't mind bearing the burden of responsibility alone. But now, after the stress of seeing Cody hurt, she felt worn down, vulnerable, frazzled.

Placing her trust in Joe's roughened hands scared her. If he hurt her son, he'd hurt her. She resented the power he had over them. She cursed her helplessness. She hated the fact that he was right. She had more to lose. And she knew it. If only she could tell him to be on his way now, this instant. But circumstances had stripped her of that ability.

She pictured her son crying, sobbing over the disappearance of his daddy. Again. How could she soothe his heartache once more? How could she manage this time? The strain of worrying over her son gnawed at her.

"Joe," she tried again. "Please, wait."

He rounded his truck.

Her heart contracted. She wanted to believe his heartfelt words. But after suffering so much disappointment, she knew she couldn't believe him till she saw him return. As if her soul cried out for this man, she knew she needed him, needed his help with her son.

If she let Joe leave on a sour note, he might change his mind, no matter what he thought or said now. She had to make sure he'd adhere to his promise. Not for her. For Cody.

"Joe, I—I...need your help." Her voice cracked. The tears she'd held at bay pressed hot against the backs of her eyes. Those words tasted bitter on her tongue. But they spoke the truth. She did need him, whether she wanted to admit it or not. She had to swallow her pride. For now. Until her son's memory returned.

Joe's footsteps faltered then stopped. Slowly he turned and faced her. He leaned against the bed of the truck, his forearms resting on the edge. The brim of his hat shaded his face. She wished she could see his eyes, gauge his anger. If body language told her anything, his fisted hands expressed his feelings with the impact of a punch.

She'd ruined everything with her quick temper and hot-headed response. The man her son thought was his father was walking right out her door and out of their lives. Her whole body shuddered with exhaustion and fear. Her hand curled around the brass doorknob to give her strength. Her shoulders sagged with the weight of her concerns.

"I'm sorry," she whispered. "So sorry." Something caught in her chest, and she released a shaky breath. "Please, Joe, come back inside."

He bent his head for a long moment. Then, with a slow, dignified cadence, he retraced his steps to her porch. He eyed her, but kept his mouth in a tight line of restraint.

"Why?" An edge sharpened his tone and cut through the last of her resolve.

She felt as if her body were caving in on itself, her weary bones folding in, her backbone dissolving. For so long she'd been strong, she'd stood alone, she'd survived. But in this one moment, it all seemed to catch up to her. Her chest ached. Tears scalded her throat. She shut her eyes tight, squeezing with every ounce of determination to hold back her tears. But they came anyway, seeping through her lashes.

In that moment, when her world fell apart, Joe touched her. He lifted her face toward his, his hand warm and insistent. His penetrating gaze stole her confidence and sent a shiver through her. Part of her wanted to lean into his hand, absorb his gentle touch, rest in his strength. But she resisted. Her heart beat wildly, like the pattering of Cody's feet when he ran through the house. Still, she couldn't move away. She stared into his eyes, mesmerized.

Then his arms came around her and pulled her against his chest. A warmth enveloped her, soothed her tattered nerves. His hands cupped her shoulders, patted her back. His voice echoed in her ear. "You've had a lot of stress tonight," he said. "It's okay."

She lifted her hand, touched the warmth of his back. He

was rock-solid. She wanted to wrap her arms around him, hold him close, rest her head against his broad shoulder, lean on him. She breathed in his scent of hay and leather, warm familiar odors that gave her a sense of security. But at the same time made her feel things she hadn't in a long while…if ever. The strange stirrings washed through her on a wave of anticipation. His strength soaked into her, fortified her. She'd always had to be strong, responsible, levelheaded. It felt good to give in to the tears, to share her burden with Joe.

Joe. His name straightened her spine. What was she doing? Leaning on him? Feeling things for a stranger—a cowboy? She didn't know him from Adam, but she knew his type. She shouldn't burden him with her problems. They were *hers* not *his*.

She pushed away from him, wiped at the dampness on her cheeks and forced her emotions back under control. "I'm okay."

Joe watched her, not sure if she said that for his or her benefit. His insides quaked. What had gotten into him? Why had he come to her aid? For crying out loud, why had he taken her into his arms?

He would forever remember the impact of her softness snuggling against him. She'd needed him. Really needed him. For a brief moment he'd helped her. It gave him a heady feeling. No one had needed him for so long. That was his own fault. He'd pushed family and friends away. But now, for some crazy reason, he wanted to be needed.

Marty rolled her lips together, as if suppressing her emotions before they got the best of her. He knew what that felt like. For so long he'd buried his own emotions. Now he felt them lurking too close to the surface.

"I'm sorry," she said. "I don't usually lose control like that."

"It's understandable. You've been through a lot in the past few hours."

"In the past few years," she muttered, and glanced away as if trying to hide the vulnerability he'd had the privilege to glimpse inside her. "I'm sorry I insulted you. I don't trust easily."

"No reason you should trust me at all." He'd never given anyone much of one before.

She shrugged. "You've given me more reasons in a few short hours than people I've known for years have." She sighed. "I honestly don't know what would be best. Maybe you should disappear. I could explain you as a dream."

"Or a nightmare?" He grinned, hoping to lighten the mood, sensing she needed it as much as he did.

She laughed then stopped, her smile fading. "Of course not." She stepped toward him, but kept her hands at her sides. "Or maybe you should come back. Until Cody's memory returns. That might be the less traumatic way to handle it. But I'd hate to ask that of you."

Her statement pricked his pride. Was *he* so awful? Was it so obvious he couldn't handle responsibility?

Her throat worked, the muscles and veins straining with emotion. "Would you mind?"

His mouth twisted with doubt. He minded, all right. But not the way she would think. He minded, because he wasn't sure he was capable of all she was asking. Uncertainty wove through him, tightening his nerves. "What would it all entail?"

"I don't know, really." She clenched her hands together. "We'd have to take it one step at a time. Follow Cody's lead. If he wakes up tomorrow, remembering everything, then we can forget having to do anything else. I'll take care of him and make him feel as secure as I can. If he still thinks you're his daddy, then I guess we'll have to go along. Of course, you won't have to stay here. With us.''

''I have a ranch,'' he said.

''Of course, you'll need to stay there and take care of it. We'll make up excuses as we go along. If you'll make a few brief appearances...'' Her gaze shifted away with uncertainty. ''Of course, I'd be happy to pay you. I don't have much, but—''

''I don't want your money.'' His tone held a decisive note.

''If you're sure...'' She offered a whisper of a smile. ''I can't imagine this will last long. I just ask that you try to consider my son's feelings at all times. No matter what you do, I have to stay here and deal with the consequences. Mop up any spills. Patch up any wounds.''

Joe's throat convulsed at the image of Cody in his mind. ''I won't hurt your boy.'' He took a step forward, sensing there was more at stake than her son. He'd glimpsed an aching wound in her, one that needed attention. It reminded him of the jagged rip in his own heart. He touched her jawline with the palm of his hand. ''I won't hurt you, either, Marty.''

His thumb caressed her cheek. Such soft, tender skin. She felt like velvet. The softness undermined his defenses better than an all-out assault. ''You don't have to be afraid of me.''

She jerked away from him. ''You're mistaken. I'm not afraid.''

His mouth twisted. ''Your ex hurt you, taught you not to trust. Something sweet and vulnerable still exists in your little boy. He still has that ability. His real daddy might have failed him, but he knows I won't. I wish you would believe that, too.''

Joe knew then he wanted to prove to this lady, to everyone else, but mostly to himself, that he could handle responsibility. He could be depended on. He needed it like the drawing of a breath of clean, fresh air. Marty needed him, too, as much as her son did.

"I'll stay as long as you need me," he added. "Then I'll be gone. For good."

"Like an angel of mercy," she said.

"I'm no angel. I'll do as you ask. Just don't expect it to be a permanent situation."

Straightening, she narrowed her gaze on him. "Of all the pigheaded things to say," she blurted. "I wasn't asking you to marry me, for God's sake."

He shook his head. "I didn't think so." A corner of his mouth pulled to the side, hinting that he might smile, but it vanished and his mouth settled back into a grim line. "You want someone dependable. I can do that. I'll be that for you. And Cody." He glanced toward the street, dark with the night as his soul with guilt. "Maybe I need it as much as you do."

He looked back at Marty. When she lifted her brows, he continued before she asked the question he wasn't willing to answer. "But temporarily. Not forever. I don't want to disappoint you in the end. I'll go my own way. I'm just giving you fair warning."

"Warning taken," she said. "Don't worry, Joe Rawlins, I won't hold any expectations in my heart. If you disappoint us, it'll just prove my theory about cowboys."

With his thumb, he nudged the brim of his hat toward his hairline. "What's that?"

"Cowboys aren't the trusting kind."

He nodded. "You're right, Marty. Don't ever forget that."

Chapter Three

"**M**omma!" Cody cried.

Scout sounded his alarm with a bark. The hair along the back of Joe's neck stood on end. Marty gripped his arm, not for support, but to hold him back.

"I'll check on him." She ran toward her son's bedroom and left Joe, halting in the den and pacing the length of the room, waiting, wondering what to do next.

As the minutes passed he veered off his single track and ambled around the room, noticing pictures of Cody, some with his mother, others with little kids. The kid with the big brown eyes had a bright, gamin smile that made his dark eyes glow. Joe conjured up an image of Marty kneeling, holding a camera and saying, "Smile."

Joe shrugged his tense neck muscles and told himself to keep his thoughts off the mom. He had no business thinking about her. No business at all.

Detouring further, he sauntered into the kitchen. A streetlight slanted through the corner window. Along the sill, several plants from ivy to aloe vera grew in an assortment of pots. He took in a breath of cinnamon apples and brown sugar. It smelled like a home. A real home. How long had it been since he'd experienced something so incredibly warm? It made him want to settle in. He reminded himself of the warning he'd given to Marty. It applied to him, as well.

He'd be true to his word. He'd hang around as long as Marty and Cody needed him. But that was all. This wasn't a forever-and-ever proposition. A coldness chilled his belly. He had no right to a home. No right to anything so wonderful. That's why he'd imprisoned himself on his ranch, away from family, friends or anyone that might bring him pleasure…anyone that might be hurt by him.

With a despondent glance at the refrigerator, he unwillingly stepped closer to examine the artwork stuck to the doors with an assortment of fruit-shaped magnets. Joe imagined Cody fashioning the pictures of stick horses and cowboys with gallon-size hats with Elmer's glue and Crayola crayons. It was clear Cody wanted to be a cowboy, like his father.

Glancing down at his old, work boots and faded jeans, Joe wondered if that wasn't the reason Cody had latched on to him as his stand-in father. His mind started thinking back to what might have been. If Samantha hadn't died. If his child had been born.

He'd denied Samantha of her right, her future as a mother. There hadn't been a day since her death that he hadn't wished it was him in that car, in that morgue, in that satin-lined coffin. He pictured what she would have looked like, holding their baby, rocking him in the chair he'd bought. On the anniversary of her death, he'd broken that chair into kindling and burned it piece by piece, trying to erase her memory from his mind. But she was forever burned in his brain, an image of a mother, never able to hold her child. His image of her now turned into an accusation. Her features twisted. *Why, Joe? Why weren't you there for me?*

A fiery band of sorrow wrapped around his heart tighter and tighter until his body became numb. Except for the dull, throbbing ache in the center of his chest. She'd never said the words. But she should have. She should have had the chance. He deserved them. He'd said them for her, over and over and over during the past five years.

He remembered the doctor telling him, "The baby your wife carried was a boy." The words, "I'm sorry," had filtered around his brain for a long time. What was the doctor sorry for? It hadn't been his fault they'd died. It hadn't been his fault that Samantha would never hold her baby. Or that a little boy wouldn't grow up, ride his first horse, kiss a girl, become a man.

It was Joe's.

Straight out of the parenthood chute, he'd disappointed his son. He'd never even had a chance to redeem himself, to show his child that he could be a good father, that he could provide for him, that he could love him. The acute pain of his loss coursed through him, saturated him with an agony that began to turn into bitterness. He had no wound to show for his pain, no disability. Only an emptiness, an aching, penetrating emptiness.

For so long he'd blocked out the pain, ignored it. But being in a real home, with a woman and her son, brought a flood of memories, and in their wake a deep cavern of loss.

Shame swept over him. He wanted to believe he'd have been a great father. But doubt burrowed deep into his soul. Samantha had gotten pregnant accidentally. She'd glowed with excitement; he'd taken the news in stride, although it had given him a burst of masculine pride. He doubted he ever would have slowed his career. He hadn't taken the time to help Samantha with the nursery. His focus hadn't swerved from rodeo. Not until...

Joe had never held his son, never told him of his love, never heard his son call him daddy.

But this little kid—Cody—had.

Plowing his fingers through his hair, Joe leaned forward, not giving himself the luxury of the softened cushions of the sofa. He rested his elbows on his knees and stared at the empty fireplace, the blackened grate. Ashes from past fires littered the bricks like the memories piling up in his mind.

Was he being asked to play daddy to a little boy who would only turn him away the day he realized Joe wasn't his father? Was this penance for his failure to protect his wife and unborn child, his failure to be there for them?

Whatever it was, he deserved it and more.

He glanced at the clock and noticed thirty minutes had passed since Marty had gone to check on Cody. Concerned, Joe tiptoed down the darkened hallway. He found Marty curled around her son. Scout snored at the end of the bed, belly up, paws stretched wide.

Joe took a soft blanket off the back of the rocker and pulled it over Marty's slender curves. His hand reached out to brush a strand of hair off her cheek. The stark contrast of his tanned fingers next to her pale skin stopped him. His heart hammered in his chest. He was being foolish. This wasn't *his* family.

With a wistful sigh, he made his way back to the den. He reclined in a leather chair and settled in for the night. He couldn't leave. Not if they might need him. He'd stay for now. He'd be here, ready to help them.

Just for tonight. Tomorrow, he'd leave.

A sharp pain gripped her neck. Marty blinked at the pale, wintry light slanting through the wooden blinds. Her eyes burned, her lids felt like sheets of sandpaper. She stifled a groan and shifted her stiff limbs. Slowly, she rotated her neck to ease out the kinks.

Staring down at her son, she breathed in the scent of his warm body nestled close to hers. His arms rested above his head. His lashes shadowed his cheeks. His chest rose and fell with each breath. How many times had she watched him sleeping, reassuring herself that he was healthy and whole? She pressed a kiss to his forehead, testing for a fever. Nothing seemed out of the ordinary. She offered a quick prayer of thanksgiving that soon he'd be bounding around the house with his usual exuberance.

A glance at her watch revealed it was still well before seven. With the crisis over, she wanted Cody to rest as long as he could. It was Sunday. No hurry in getting up. They could miss Sunday school this once.

Giving in to a yawn, she pushed herself out of her son's bed. Her movement woke Scout, who rolled to his side and looked at her imploringly. He thumped his tail against the mattress. She smiled and rubbed his velvety head. "Come on, boy."

Walking out of the room, she stretched and sucked in a deep, invigorating breath. A warm, inviting scent of stout coffee and cinnamon biscuits caught her attention. Her brow wrinkled with confusion. She stared down the hallway. What on earth?

Joe. Oh, God. She'd forgotten all about him.

She'd gone to comfort Cody. The minutes had ticked by like long, lonely days, and she'd grown sleepy. When Cody drifted off, she had, too. Had Joe stayed the night? How could she have forgotten he was in her house?

Padding down the carpeted hallway in her socks, she heard the clatter of pans and the rush of water in the sink coming from the kitchen. She grasped Scout's collar and put him out in the backyard for his business. The greasy odor of bacon reached her before she rounded the corner to the kitchen. She stopped, struck by the sight in front of her.

Joe stood at the gas stove, his back to her. Bacon sizzled and popped in the frying pan. Her gaze remained riveted to him. His ruffled hair had a cowlick where he must have rested his head during the night. Where had he slept? On the couch? In a bed? Her skin tightened with awareness at the thought of him sliding his long frame between her sheets.

Shaking off the uncomfortable thoughts, she gave him a quick once-over. His starched shirt had given in to wrinkles. It hung from his shoulders around his slim hips, untucked. The material shifted enticingly over his well-defined muscles each time he moved or lifted the pan off the element to turn the bacon. He seemed sure and capable, confident in the chore that had always been too much of a burden for her ex-husband.

Morning sunlight poured through the window and caught those golden strands in his thick hair. Decidedly handsome in a rumpled, sexy way, his presence disturbed her even more. Last night he'd taken control, irritated her. Today, his shoulders seemed wider, his legs longer, the faded denim molding to their contours. He looked as natural in her kitchen as he did in jeans.

Something stirred in her belly, and it scared the stuffing out of her. She blamed the provocative sensation on a severe case of hunger. It was better than the alternative—blatant attraction. Yes, Joe was a handsome cowboy with startling blue eyes and a lazy smile that affected her far too much. She didn't need a cowboy, though. She'd had one. Flint's boyish grin had snagged her interest a long time ago, but the cold reality of his empty charm had immunized her against sexy cowboys. Or had it?

During their marriage, she'd tried to give Flint more

responsibilities, but he'd complained that she'd dumped her burdens on him. When he'd finally left for good, she'd realized her largest burden had been lifted from her shoulders. She hated to admit she'd been as ready for the marriage to end. Poor Cody hadn't been ready to let go, though. Could his need have triggered his selective amnesia?

If so, that made it imperative that she get rid of Joe as soon as possible. What if Cody got used to him? Continued to think of him as his daddy? As much as Flint's immaturity had annoyed her, he was still her son's father. He always would be. No matter what.

What truly frightened her was how easy it could be for *her* to depend on Joe. He hadn't bucked responsibility as Flint had. He'd jumped right in, taken action, done more than anyone could have asked for him to do. He'd made her feel less alone. He'd offered her his shoulder to cry on. He'd been a friendly face in the midst of her fear. And now he was stirring up a tempting breakfast. Eventually, though, Joe would leave and she'd be alone again, carrying her own responsibilities. Would they seem heavier after this reprieve? She didn't want to find out.

Finger-combing her hair back, the tangles snagged her fingers. Suddenly aware of her disheveled appearance, she glanced down at her untucked shirt and crumpled jeans. Her appearance matched his, and it instantly made the whole situation too intimate. She wanted—needed—to feel more in control. A shower or at least a change of clothes would help. Hoping to sneak out of the kitchen before he saw her, she took a step backward.

Her stomach rumbled. Loudly this time. A sound a deaf man would have found hard to ignore. She clamped a hand over the emptiness and dodged out of sight behind the den wall.

"Mornin'." Joe's voice stopped her in her tracks. It had

a sleepy, crackling quality that reminded her of a campfire on a brisk morning.

Caught, she decided to face him rather than run and hide. She stepped back into his line of vision and gave him a shy smile. "Good morning to you."

He turned around and gave her a jaunty grin. Her stomach flipped over. His hair fell lazily over his brow. Her flowered oven mitt covered one of his hands, making her smile. His blue gaze, however, lingered on her, coasting down her length, making her insides tingle with an unfamiliar heat. "You look good."

A nervous laugh bubbled out of her. "Yeah, right." She touched her hand to her face. "With smeared makeup, hair like a bush, and wrinkled clothes."

His grin widened, the brackets around his mouth deepening, his teeth flashing white against his tanned skin, his eyes crinkling at the corners. Those crystal-blue eyes emanated a warmth that made her toes curl toward the tiled floor. "Well, we both look like we've been—" His eyes darkened, a cloud of desire deepening the color to a stormy sea. He cleared his throat with a cough. "Sleeping in our clothes. What I meant was, you look more relaxed today." His gaze shifted back to the stove and the bacon.

She nodded, his implication tightening her nerves and sharpening her awareness of him.

"I take it Cody's feeling better?"

"He's still asleep."

"Good. Did you have a rough night?"

"Not too bad. I woke up periodically and checked on him to make sure he could wake up. That's what the doctor told me to do, anyway." She tilted her head, curiosity getting the better of her. "Where'd you sleep?"

"In the den. That big leather chair in there is comfortable. I made myself at home." He cut his gaze toward her. "I hope that was all right. I waited, after you went to check on Cody. When you didn't return, I found you sleeping. I didn't want to disturb you."

She felt uneasy as she imagined him watching her sleep. "You could have gone on home," she said, wishing at this moment that he had. "We were fine."

"I know. But I wanted to be here." A muscle ticked along the square edge of his jaw. "If you needed anything."

She bit back a sharp retort that she could care for herself and her son. He wasn't saying she couldn't. Something in his tone, in the way he wouldn't look at her, told her it was a risky step for him to admit he cared. In any way, shape, or form.

"I appreciate your help last night."

He shrugged. "Didn't do anything that someone else wouldn't have done."

She doubted that. "Well, I couldn't have gotten through it without you."

His gaze met hers, locked and held. "Yes, you could have. You're resourceful."

Her face grew warm from his praise, his confidence. Flint had never acknowledged her abilities, never thanked her for doing what he called women's work—such as cooking, cleaning and helping to bring home the metaphorical bacon. A year or two, she'd actually made more than he had, with her working as a teacher's aide. That hadn't set too well, either.

Now she glimpsed a vulnerability in Joe, a streak of concern and caring that ran deep into his heart. In that instant he became the most attractive man she'd ever met. She rubbed her palms against the backside of her jeans. Uncomfortable with her private admission and Joe's kindness, she glanced at the mixing bowls.

"Breakfast is almost ready." He clasped a strip of bacon

between tongs and turned it over. "You and I can eat. I'll fix Cody's eggs when he gets up."

"Oh, that's not necessary." She moved forward. "You didn't have to go to all this trouble." She reached for the metal tongs.

He turned another sizzling strip. "Sure I did. I was starving." His mouth curved up at the corner. "And you must be, too."

Heat crept up her neckline. So, he'd heard her stomach rumble, not just her poor attempt at escape. Her hand touched her empty stomach again. "Well, then let me do something."

"Nope." He stood in her way like a fortress blocking access to her stove. She had no choice but to let him continue or else push him bodily out of the kitchen. Not that she'd have much of a chance manhandling this cowboy. And she wasn't willing to risk touching his broad frame to get her way. She had an odd feeling her attempt would backfire, and she'd get burned.

"You just relax," he said. "Have a cup of coffee. Enjoy the morning. I like to cook."

Surprised, she blinked. "You like to cook?"

"Sure. And I do dishes, too."

She remembered again her ex's proclamation that cooking and cleaning and caring for kids was women's work. She hadn't experienced his chauvinistic streak until after she'd promised to love and honor.

Intrigued by this man who seemed different, she said, "You mean, you don't think it's a woman's job?"

"I don't think of it as work. Except for the cleaning-up part. You're welcome to that, if you like." He gave her a teasing wink that made her stomach clench. "Besides, most of the great chefs are men."

Her backbone stiffened. "Are you saying women *can't* cook?"

He chuckled, the sound rumbling out of his chest and dissolving her irritation. He waggled his head back and forth. "You sure want to get your dander up this morning. Nope. I'm not saying that."

She crossed her arms over her chest and leaned back against the center island, which was cluttered with mixing bowls and measuring spoons and dotted with flour. She watched his culinary skills with grudging admiration for the ease with which he handled a frying pan. "Then you're a real man of the nineties."

He shrugged off her compliment. "Had to learn or starve. Of course, some might say I'm from the nineteenth century. But I don't mind. Maybe I would have felt more at home on some range, boiling my coffee on an open fire, cooking biscuits in a Dutch oven."

He opened the oven and peered inside. She caught a glimpse over his shoulder of honey-brown biscuits, plump and full, sprinkled with cinnamon. The warm buttery scent made her mouth water.

"But it's easier this modern way." He set the metal tongs on the ceramic spoon in the center of the stove. He edged past her, his arm brushing hers, making her too aware of his size, his presence, his warmth. Yet he seemed oblivious to the way he affected her. Of course, why would he be attracted to her? What with the way she looked this morning and how she'd acted like a shrew last night. She pushed a lock of hair back behind one ear.

"How do you like yours?" Opening the refrigerator, he pulled out a carton of eggs. "Scrambled? Fried? Over easy?"

His lazy smile disarmed her. Her mind floundered. Such an easy decision, but she couldn't seem to make it. Not with him staring at her. With those eyes. Those blue-tinted eyes that looked as clear as the sun shimmering off a lake. Her reaction to him surprised and unnerved her. What had happened to her? You'd think she'd been the one conked on the head.

"You've done enough already. Let me do the eggs." She had to do something to get her mind off this man and his eyes. She grabbed an egg out of the open carton and it slipped right through her fingers. It hit the floor with a crack. The yolk oozed out, spreading over the tile.

"Dammit." She met Joe's amused stare.

"I don't do floors," he said, handing her a paper towel. She knelt and cleaned up her mess. "Maybe you need some coffee to wake up. I'll get you a cup."

He opened the cabinet above the sink and pulled out the mug her son had given her last Mother's Day. Joe's familiarity with her kitchen bothered her. She plucked the cup out of his hands, her fingers brushing his. He had work hands, hard, calloused, weathered. She turned away sharply, avoiding the way her stomach curled into a tight ball at his slightest touch. Grabbing the carafe out of the coffeemaker, she poured a generous portion into her cup.

"Do you need sugar or cream?" he asked, his voice too masculine, too inviting, too close.

She stepped away from him. "No, th—" Hot liquid sloshed over the rim and burned her hand. "Oh."

He moved closer. "Here, let me see."

"N-no, I'm okay."

But he wouldn't take her word for it. Again, he took charge. Against her will, she let him. Taking the mug from her, he cupped her hand in his. His touch was gentle, as if he cradled a mewling kitten. His gaze studied the red, angry mark across the back of her hand.

"Hold on," he said. "I'll take care of you—" His eyes met hers, wide blue oceans of emotional turmoil, and her heart rolled over. "Er, this," he amended.

She caught his blunder, surprise and embarrassment. And yet, she held those sweet words in her heart. No one had ever said that to her. She'd never craved a knight in shining armor, a man to come to her rescue, never asked for it. Or had she? Is that what she'd really wanted from Flint?

With her ex, she'd quickly learned what to expect—nothing. She'd had to be strong. But what of this man? Her heart told her not to trust, not yet. She never wanted to feel that raw disappointment again.

Staring into Joe's eyes, something electric flashed between them. Something she couldn't define or explain. Something she had to avoid.

She reminded herself he was here for her son's sake. That was all.

He glanced away first. Focusing on her hand, he blew softly across her burned flesh. "You need to put something on this."

Abruptly, he turned off the burner under the bacon. Without a glance in her direction, he whipped a pocket-knife out of his hip pocket and clipped off a stalk of the aloe vera plant on the window ledge. Holding the oozing leaf, he looked at her. "Do you have any bandages?"

"Of course. I have a five-year-old." She pushed away from the counter. "I'll get them."

"Nope. You stay put." His take-charge attitude grated on her nerves, yet at the same time gave her a sense of security. She didn't know which reaction should scare her more. "You're a walking disaster this morning. Just tell me where."

His quick wink softened the truth of his words. She gave him the directions to the utility room and the location of the superhero bandages. He returned with a smile. Once again, he cupped her hand, smoothed the aloe vera onto the burn with deliberate tenderness and covered it with a bright yellow bandage, careful not to place the sticky tabs on her sensitive flesh.

"How does that feel?" he asked, his voice husky.

Too good, she thought, as he held her hand gently. Her body tingled all over, awareness rippling through her. She took in a steadying breath and absorbed his scent. The masculine odor reminded her of a brisk walk in the bright sunlight and stirred her senses awake. Her body flushed in response, as if she'd sunbathed and had been kissed by the warm Texas sun.

Kissed. The word lingered in her mind. Her gaze dropped to Joe's mouth. His lips looked firm and sensual. Her stomach fluttered at the thought of those lips pressing against hers. The idea of his shadowy beard teasing her mouth made her pulse skitter.

She jerked her attention back to her hand and curled her fingers into a fist. "It's fine, thanks."

He stepped away from her, a strange look deepening the lines in his face.

"I better see to breakfast." He edged around her and stuffed his hand back into the flowered mitt to pull the biscuits out of the oven.

"You seem to have done this before," she said, running her finger along the neat bandage he'd fashioned.

"You mean, cooking?"

"That, too, but I meant patching people up."

"Not really." He shrugged. "I rodeoed."

The reminder brought her crazy response to him back under control. His succinct statement explained more in two words than a medical journal. He'd rodeoed. Therefore, he'd been injured. He'd probably seen many more. And cowboys never quit. Unless an injury put them in the hospital or morgue. They wrapped their wrists, ribs or knees and rode as if there were no tomorrow. She focused on that fact. He was a cowboy, through and through.

Just like Flint. Although her ex had never bandaged her

injuries or even diapered Cody. Flint had taken care of himself. That was all he'd been capable of.

Her gaze settled on Joe once more. There was no reason to become attached to this cowboy. He'd be going. Just like the last.

Like a vulture seeking a weak spot, a thought circled around her mind—Joe had quit the rodeo. She remembered the press about it years ago. Maybe he was different. But that didn't settle her jumbled nerves.

"Daddy makes gooder biscuits than you, Momma." Cody crammed another butter-laden biscuit into his mouth. A dollop of strawberry jam seeped out and landed on his plate.

Joe watched Marty's tight smile. He'd touched her earlier. That had been a mistake. One he'd regret for many nights to come. Worse, he'd promised to take care of her. Where had that come from? Had he been the one to suffer amnesia? He knew better than anyone that he wasn't capable of taking care of anyone but himself.

And sometimes he didn't do a very good job of that.

He'd worn out his welcome here. It was time to move on. Before it was too late. Or was it already?

"You know, Cody," he said, "since you seem to be feeling better, maybe I better head on to that rodeo." Joe stood from the table and pushed his chair in. "Mind if I leave you with the dishes, Marty?"

The little boy's brow crinkled, but his mother gave him an affirming nod. "We'll be fine here," she said. "Don't worry about us."

"Can't you skip the rodeo just this once?" Cody whined.

Purposefully not looking at the boy's deep brown eyes, Joe shook his head and walked into the den. "Not if we want to eat around here."

He turned and gave Marty a wink to assure her he would play along with the charade since Cody obviously still thought he was his father. He glanced at his watch, wishing he had a rodeo to escape to. His blood froze in his veins like ice. Would he have been eager to return to the road if his wife and son had lived? He didn't want to know the answer to that.

"If I hurry I can just make the last event," he rasped.

"Well, be careful," Marty said, standing in the archway.

Joe picked his hat up off the couch, settled it on his head and ruffled Cody's hair. "You be good, cowboy. Take care of your momma and no more ridin' rank sheep for a while. Okay?"

"Okay." His eyes shone as he looked up at Joe. "Can you teach me to ride your horse, Daddy?"

Joe glanced at Marty and caught the concern in her frozen features. "Let's wait and see what the doctor says. I don't think you should be riding anything...horses, bulls, sheep or even Scout...for a while."

"But I'd be okay with you there."

His heart contracted. God, he wished that were true. But the simple fact was, he'd already let this kid fall once. Dependability had never been his strong suit. It was time to go before anything else happened. He moved to the door. "Y'all take care."

"Thanks," Marty said, opening the door for him. "For everything."

"Not a problem." He slipped a piece of paper out of his back pocket. "Here's the phone number where I'll be." He gave her a pointed stare, hoping she understood it was his home number. Their fingers brushed as she took the slip of paper from him. Her soft skin and softer gaze made him offer, "Call if you need anything."

Cody trudged to the door. His face long and sad. Joe

chucked him on the chin. The bump on his forehead had shrunk, but the bruise was still dark and violent. "I'll be home—er, back in a few days, cowboy."

The boy nodded and slipped his hand into his mother's. His little shoulders sagged, telling Joe more about the kid's father than he wanted to know. Flint must have left often and rarely returned. Joe had been like that once.

Knowing he shouldn't, but unable to resist, he knelt and opened his arms to Cody. "How about a hug for the road?"

"I thought you were in a hurry." The little boy's voice wavered.

"Never in too much of a hurry for you."

Cody rushed into his arms and snuggled close. He gave Joe a squeeze around the neck and a peck on the cheek. The innocence and sweetness behind the gesture made his throat burn with regret. That warm little body made Joe ache for something he couldn't have…his own son.

"'Bye, Daddy. Come home soon." Those words squeezed Joe's heart.

God, he almost wished he could come back and pretend this was his family, his home. But it wasn't. It never would be.

Giving the brim of his hat a tug, he nodded and turned to go. He didn't belong here. The cozy family environment reminded him of how much he'd missed, how wrong he'd been. Before he made it down the front steps, Cody called out to him, "Aren't you gonna kiss Momma 'bye?"

His feet stopped of their own accord, even when his head and heart told him to keep walking and pretend he hadn't heard. Slowly, he turned. His gaze met Marty's wide brown eyes. A hot blush stole up her neckline and flamed her cheeks.

"Cody—" her voice pitched higher "—Daddy's in a hurry."

"But he said—"

"That's right, cowboy." Joe stepped toward her, surprised by his own actions as much as she was. He couldn't explain it. He wasn't sure he wanted to. But damn, he wanted a kiss goodbye. Even if it was a pretend one. Even if it meant nothing to Marty. For some reason that he couldn't comprehend, it meant something to him. They'd been through a lot together in the past twenty-four hours. Tomorrow, if Cody's memory returned, that fragile bond they'd shared would be severed. But today, he could pretend even for a moment that this was *his* family.

Wariness glinted in Marty's eyes. She tilted her chin, giving him access to her cheek. Determined to keep her from stepping away from him, he gripped her shoulders. He needed this more than he cared to admit. He'd shared moments with Marty, moments of concern and fear and tenderness that had left them both vulnerable. He needed to share this. Lifting her chin, he tilted his mouth toward hers, shuttered his eyes and imagined her smiling. For him. This once.

His gaze dropped to her mouth. Her lips were full, sensuous, as if ripe with sweet nectar. He pressed his mouth to hers. At first, she stiffened, but a slow warmth merged between them and seeped into his soul. She yielded to his persistence. Her softness gentled his heart.

This wasn't a farewell. He'd be back. Whether he wanted to or not. He couldn't say goodbye. Not yet. Not now.

Chapter Four

A hot flush surged through her. Marty felt as if every pore in her body had opened with longing, each heated thought centered on Joe. Her lips tingled from where he'd kissed her. She pressed a finger to the sensitized flesh. With her heart pounding in her chest, she watched him drive away, the truck's muffler emitting a cloud of smoke. She hoped his impact on her would disintegrate into a whisper of nothing as easily as the exhaust.

But she doubted that.

He was not a man easily forgotten. He'd swooped into her life, taking charge, giving her a shoulder to lean on. His kiss had awakened a part of her that she'd thought had died. Had she ever been kissed with such gentle passion? Her ex-husband had "claimed" her by grabbing and planting one on her. But had he ever been tender? Sweet? Softly tempting? His mouth had never toyed with hers. Not like Joe's.

Joe's mouth had hovered over hers, not with hesitation, but with deliberate purpose, teasing her with his warm breath, making clear his intentions. He'd held on to her arms, not giving her room for escape. Strangely enough, she hadn't wanted to evade him, she'd wanted to lean into his welcoming heat, his strength.

His scent, a mixture of leather and tangy masculinity, had surrounded, lured, enticed her. Her senses had drawn in the sweet, mellow taste of orange marmalade and the stronger hint of coffee. His gentle touch had weakened her knees.

Now with the morning chill cooling her heated response, she still felt weak. From his kiss. From her need.

She wanted his strong arms wrapped around her, pulling her tight against his broad chest, blocking out everything. Except her and him. If only for a few crazy seconds.

She hadn't been with anyone since Flint. She hadn't even looked in another man's direction. Until now.

As daring as a bolt of lightning, Joe Rawlins had shocked her back to an awareness of male and female, the subtle nuances, the familiar differences that mattered so much. His hardness. Her softness. His need. Her desire.

With her longing for more, he'd left without a glance over his shoulder, making her doubt their brief, intimate contact had affected him as it had her. Had he seen it as a duty, as a performance for Cody's benefit?

Now with her body as vibrant as the sun, radiating a rare heat on this wintry day, she offered a silent prayer that he remembered his promise to her son. With a twinge of guilt, she realized her wish wasn't entirely for Cody's sake.

That unnerved her more than his kiss had.

Tilted off center, she stood unmoving, not daring even a step backward inside the house. Her hand pressed against her chest as if trying to still the erratic beat of her heart. What had happened to her? All in that fleeting instant. It was as if she'd been numb...dead. And with a brief kiss,

Joe had awakened her to a whole new world, full of spinning, churning, swooning sensations she'd forgotten over the last few years.

But she wouldn't lose her head...or her heart. Not over a cowboy. Not again.

"Momma?" Cody tugged on her sleeve.

Pulled out of her kaleidoscope of emotions, she glanced at her tiny son. The January chill seeped through her clothes. "We shouldn't be standing out here in this weather." Although she could have used the cool air to bring her temperature down a notch. "Let's get you inside. You need to rest."

"But, Momma, I'm not tired."

Glad for the distraction from her jumbled thoughts, she patted his shoulder and urged him inside. "You should be."

"You know what?" he asked, his wide brown eyes full of hope.

She brushed a lock of hair off his brow. Only a tiny bump remained on his forehead, but an ugly purple bruise had risen, marring his delicate skin. "What, sweetheart?"

"Daddy loves us." His mouth curled into a contagious grin.

Her mouth congealed into a parody of a smile. Her heart contracted with a pain that threatened to never cease.

"When will he come home?"

"Soon, baby, soon," she said, her voice as faint as her heartbeat was frantic. She curled her hand around the slip of paper Joe had given her, burying it in her palm. The paper crinkled beneath the pressure of her fingers. She tossed his phone number in the nearest trash can.

She wouldn't call.

And she hoped Joe had already forgotten about her and Cody.

Somehow she'd have to figure out a way to pacify her son. Alone.

"Momma, I need lunch money," Cody said, hooking his yellow book bag over his tiny shoulder. He looked smaller than usual, bundled inside a wool jacket, knit cap and plump mittens. An urge to pull him back into the car and keep him close to her the rest of the day washed over her.

But the doctor had given his okay for Cody to return to school on Monday. Like any overly concerned parent, Marty had her doubts. She knew they were caused more by her insecurities than Cody's injuries.

He stuck his hand, palm up, through the open window, waiting for his lunch money.

"All right." She nodded and reached behind the seat of her car, searching for her purse. Her hand groped Cody's toy horse, a well-loved book, and an empty fast-food sack. Swiveling around, she stared at the empty back seat.

Where was her purse?

Her mind swam with possibilities. Had she put it in the car this morning? She couldn't remember. They'd been in a rush. When had she seen it last? She tapped her forehead, hoping to jog loose a faint memory. She'd had it at the rodeo. She remembered holding it against her stomach when Cody had ridden that damn sheep. She vaguely recalled rummaging in her purse at the hospital for insurance cards and identification.

Her pulse skittered to a halt.

She'd put it in Joe's truck, behind the seat, while she'd held Cody on the way back to her car, her keys already anxiously in her hand. She had been eager to get Cody safely home and in bed and impatient to say goodbye to Joe. For good. But he'd followed her home, helped her carry her son into the house. And her purse had been forgotten in his truck!

"Momma?" Cody prodded.

"Uh, sorry, baby. I, uh, forgot my—" Her heart hammered, knowing she'd have to see Joe again and that she'd now have to track him down. "Oh, here, Cody." She dug in the ashtray full of coins for a few quarters. "Here you go, sweetheart. Give this to your teacher for your lunch. Be careful."

Nodding, Cody gave her a final smile. "See ya."

"'Bye, honey, have a good day. I'll pick you up this afternoon," she called after him, but he'd already skipped around the corner of the brick building and entered the door for kindergartners.

Marty leaned forward, purposefully knocking her head lightly against the steering wheel, and cursed. Why had she been so stupid? Because her son had needed her. What was she supposed to do now? She fisted the cold plastic circular frame.

She'd have to call him. She had no choice.

It wouldn't be a problem. That is, if she hadn't thrown his number out with the trash. Nor would it bother him. After all, he expected her to call. But how would *she* handle seeing him again, wondering about his kiss, if it had meant anything to him? Oh, God. She fell back against the seat. She wished she had Cody's temporary amnesia.

Joe had the flu. Or at least a few of the symptoms. The thought of food made him nauseous. In the middle of the night, he'd awakened, his skin clammy with sweat. He'd stared into the darkness, listening to the silence crashing over him, waiting for the unforgiving light. Ghostly faces haunted him. One face so familiar…yet so far away and growing ever more distant. The other he'd conjured up out of thin air. That tiny, sweet, trusting baby face broke his heart. The image shifted and changed into the shape of Cody, smiling and calling him daddy.

Sleepless nights were not unusual for him, not since....

He'd learned to live with the emptiness, the pounding silence, the guilt. It hadn't been easy. He'd come to think of it as punishment. As a way to live, no longer feeling, no longer wanting. But now he faced something infinitely more difficult.

Already, his chest grew tight, his lungs trapping each breath at the thought of never seeing Marty and Cody again. How could they have become a part of him so quickly? His first mistake had been to care. He should have dumped them at the hospital and run as if the devil were after him. His second mistake had been to offer Cody a hug. The memory of the little body, clasping him with tiny hands on his shoulders, gripped his heart with a sharp pain. He'd never realized, even with all his imaginings of his own child, how tender and wonderful a kid could be. His final and worse mistake had been to kiss her.

He'd felt Marty's hesitation, her wariness, a palpable fear. Had Flint wounded her with his callous ways? Had he destroyed her ability to give love and receive it? Joe remembered how she'd pushed him away, determined to take care of herself and her son. She needed no man, especially not some worthless rancher like Joe.

But for one insane second during their kiss, he'd felt her respond. Like a rose opening, she'd softened, relaxed, unfolded her protective petals enough to let him in. It had been too much. He'd broken away. His knees had felt as weak as a newborn colt's as he'd walked to his pickup. With every ounce of determination he possessed, he'd forced each step away from her.

How could he go back now? How could he endure more torture?

He prayed Cody regained his memory. Then Marty wouldn't call. And he wouldn't have to see her again.

With that one ounce of hope, he'd faced the oncoming day. Earlier than usual, he'd dragged himself out of bed and out to do his chores. Work kept his crazy thoughts corralled. He wished he was on the road, having to concentrate on the next bull he'd ride. But he was stuck here, trapped with his disconcerting memories.

In the pale light within the barn, he lifted a bale of hay, his knees bent, his arms straining, and crossed the length of wooden shelter. A soft grunt escaped his lips as he dropped it on top of another square bale. Tiny bits of straw whirled around him. With a cough, he stepped back. His breath puffed like a white cloud in the cold January air. The chill on his bare arms made his skin sticky from sweat.

Retracing his steps, he kept his mind on his chores. With his thoughts occupied, the ache in his limbs eased. Exerting so much effort, he began to think about lunch.

His truck sat parked in the wide doorway of the barn. He glanced through the opening, over the bed and beyond the cab to the world beyond his tiny universe that revolved around feeding cattle, pulling calves, and cutting, baling and hauling hay. The winter sky looked deathly pale, trapped between a dreary blue and a dismal gray.

An unusual sight caught his attention and made the hair at the base of his neck stand on end. A visitor, a shadowy silhouette, sat inside a compact blue car in the driveway.

No one came calling anymore.

He'd discouraged that, starting with the local church-goers bringing casseroles and cakes, brisket, beans, and mounds of potatoes after his wife had died. It had seemed ironic to be given something to nourish him when all he'd wanted to do was starve.

Then the women had come. Lonely women, desperate women, women who knew he was hurting and grieving and who wanted to ease his pain. But he'd deserved the pain. And he'd sent them away.

Curious and wary, he ambled toward the parked car. He yanked off his leather gloves and tucked them into his hip pocket. He hadn't bothered putting on his sheepskin jacket, and the cool air chilled his exposed skin where he'd rolled the sleeves of his flannel shirt past his elbows.

When the car door opened and a familiar face gave him a shy smile, his heart tripped over itself. Surprised and shaken, he paused. Alighting with the deftness of a teenage girl, Marty stood in the driveway. She wore snug jeans and a bulky coat. She left the car door open, as if she needed a quick escape. He whipped off his hat and rubbed his forearm over his brow. Bits of straw scratched his skin, but he only noticed her. Her warm brown eyes. The blush coloring her cheeks. Her smile, brighter than the bleak sun that shone on her thick, black hair.

"Hello," she called, her brow crinkling.

"Marty," he said, suddenly filled with worry. "Is there something wrong?"

"No." The word exploded from her. "No." She softened her tone. "I mean, Cody's fine. He's in school."

"Good. Has he, um, regained his memory?"

She shook her head. The distress in her dark gaze matched the churning emotions inside him. She clasped her hands in front of her, settled one on the black rim of the car door, before finally crossing her arms over her chest.

"How did you find me? I'm not listed in the Yellow Pages."

"You mean under Cowboy Willing To Help?"

He chuckled. "Did you try to call?"

"No," she admitted. "I thought it would be simpler this way."

His blood ran cold. It would be hard enough for him to

walk out of their lives, but if she kicked him out.... His
ego balked. Anger spurred his pride.

Her gaze shifted then darted back, as if she'd made a
decision. "I called the rodeo association. They hooked me
up with the doctor who worked on Cody. He said he didn'
know if you still lived out here or not."

The eagerness at seeing her faded, and an edginess took
its place. "Are you cold?" he asked. He slapped himsel
mentally for standing and gawking like a drooling teena-
ger. "Of course, you're cold." He sniffed the frigid air
"It's only thirty degrees. Sometimes I'm as dense as one
of the bulls in my pasture. Come on inside."

"Really, I shouldn't..." Her voice trailed off. She met
his gaze. Something in the chocolate depths gentled. "Jus
for a minute, then."

A lightness lifted the heavy worry off his heart. He led
her up the porch steps and opened the front door. The
blinds covering the pane-glass windows slapped against
the oak. He watched her enter his house, tentative, almost
shy, as she edged into the darkened room. He brushed past
her in his haste to open shades and curtains and flip on a
ceiling light. Dust particles twirled in the weak light slanting through the speckled windows. He held his hat in his
hands and waited for her to move forward.

When she didn't, he said, "Can I take your coat?"

She shook her head. "I can't stay long."

"Have a seat." He gestured toward the lonely sofa. "I'l
get you something to drink. Uh, what would you like?"
He sidestepped to the kitchen as she walked into the living
room and settled on the edge of the sofa cushions like a
bird perched and ready for flight. The light of the refrigerator made him squint at the emptiness inside. "I've got
some orange juice," he muttered, unscrewing the lid and
wrinkling his nose. "Or maybe not. How about water?"

"Joe, I'm fine." She couldn't stay anyway. She shouldn't be here now. But she wouldn't leave yet.

Joe returned to the living room, looking as anxious as an old hound dog on a night with a full moon. Tension rippled through her, tightening her muscles as she clenched her hands in her lap. She wished she could go, but the eager look in his eyes made her think of Cody when he wanted desperately to please her. For some reason, Joe tugged at her heart.

And she couldn't turn away.

Rubbing his hands on the back of his jeans, he moved toward her, but kept his distance. At her silent invitation, he lowered himself onto the cushion at the opposite end of the sofa.

"How are you holding up?" he asked.

"Fine." Her gaze shifted to a broken cobweb that drifted in the warm gust of air from a vent. "And you?"

"Fine."

The awkward silence swelled between them. She wondered if she should have said Cody regained his memory and dismissed Joe from their lives with one easy lie. Or maybe she should simply set a few basic rules, barring any more kisses. Or would that put more emphasis on the kiss? Her mind spun with uncertainty until an answer settled over her thoughts like the thick covering of dust over one of his lampshades.

"I tried to call." His statement startled her.

"You did?"

"Last night. And then again this morning."

She drew her bottom lip between her teeth. "I turned the ringer off on the phone. Cody had a headache. And this morning I drove him to school."

"Do you have an answering machine?" he asked. "If not, I have an old one that I don't use anymore. You could have it. That way if I call, I could leave you a message. I'd say it so Cody would think it's—"

"His daddy?"

His brow knitted into tiny furrowed lines. His angular face sharpened with frustration.

She plowed her fingers through her hair. How long could they do this? How long would she have to depend on this man?

Abruptly she stood. "Joe, I came out here today…"

The words died on her lips. She saw an intense pain deep in his blue eyes. It was raw, jagged and piercing. She cursed herself for not being able to end this thing now, right here, forever.

"It's about that kiss, isn't it?" he said, his tone flat.

"What makes you think that?" Her voice squeaked. Heat tingled her face. She sank back down onto the sofa, her knees wobbly.

His gaze focused on her, his eyes narrowing. He edged closer to her, shifting on the sofa. "Look, I didn't mean anything by it. I thought it would look strange if two married people didn't want to kiss."

She nodded, unable to get any words past the lump in her throat.

"I figured Cody's insecure about his daddy being gone. Maybe if he feels safe, his memory will come back."

And you'll be free of this burden. That thought burned in her mind. Joe, like Flint, didn't want anything to do with them, either. Responsibility to a cowboy was like a heavy saddle on a wild Mustang. They would always buck against it. She had to remember that.

"It won't happen again," he said with firm conviction in his voice. His gaze dropped to her mouth and made her insides tighten. "Unless…"

"Unless?" Her stomach rolled over. She realized at that moment that she wanted him to kiss her again. More fully.

She stole a glance at his wide mouth, remembering its effect on her. As quickly as they'd arisen, she stomped down those irrational thoughts. She wouldn't get involved with Joe. She wouldn't get involved with *any* cowboy.

"Unless Cody says something. Like before."

"Oh." She felt as if heat radiated from her. Crossing her arms over her chest, she wrestled her desires under control. "If that happens, then we should make it a kiss on the cheek."

His intense gaze bore into her. "If that's what you want."

"It is," she said, her voice too soft, too doubtful. Taking in a skimpy breath, she stood. "I forgot my purse in your truck."

He blinked and rose to his feet. "Your purse? I didn't see it."

She moved a step away from him, needing space, needing to leave. "I set it in the back, in the jump seat."

He nodded. "It's still there, then. I'll get it for you."

As if he, too, were eager to leave the kissing conversation behind, he grabbed his hat off the dusty coffee table and headed toward the door. She noted his broad shoulders, the sweat stains along his back. She wondered why this gentle, caring cowboy was still single. Or was he? Was he just being nice? Suddenly it seemed paramount for her to know.

"Joe?" She stopped him before he plunged out into the cold, frosty morning.

"Hmm?" He paused, his hand on the door.

Her gaze swept over the barren, shabby room that looked more like a tomb than someone's living room. The air smelled stale, lifeless. A shriveled brown plant remained on the kitchen table. She chose her words carefully. "Are you married or seeing anyone?" Her heart raced. "I mean, I didn't ask you the other night if your helping us intruded on your personal life."

"No," he said, his tone solemn, "I'm not married. Or anything else."

She could have kicked herself after he'd left, closing the door softly behind him, for her insensitivity. She'd charged right into that one like a bull into a china closet. Joe probably thought... What did it matter? But she knew it did. It mattered a lot.

Standing alone in his living room, she studied his place more thoroughly. No pictures adorned tabletops. No television collected dust. No mementos, no trophies. Nothing decorated the room in any way. All color had been eliminated, except for the dull brown shade of the paneled walls and the drab beige sofa.

Did Joe have family? Connections? Loved ones? Or was he totally alone? Had that been why he was so willing to help her and Cody?

Her heart contracted. This strong, responsible, well-meaning cowboy seemed to have no one. But her and Cody. How could that be?

With a cold brush of air, he walked back inside, closing the door on the gusts of wind. "Found it. Good thing I did, too. Otherwise, I might have gotten myself in trouble on my next date." He gave her a friendly wink. "It's getting colder. Looks like a storm could be on its way. I heard earlier today there's a possibility of sleet."

"They always say that. And chances are that it'll sleet and snow in Oklahoma and that's as close as it will get to Texas."

"Could be. But you shouldn't risk it."

"I won't. I have to pick up Cody in a while anyway." She headed toward the door, retrieving her purse from him and tucking it under her arm. "Joe." She stopped beside him, turned and realized she was closer than she'd expected.

He was staring down at her, his gaze shuttered, his emotions closed. She wished she knew what he was thinking, if he was lonely, if he cared that they'd kissed, if he wanted to kiss her again.

"Do you miss rodeoing?" she asked, wanting to know why a championship cowboy was alone on a small ranch.

"Sometimes." His lips compressed into a thin line.

"Ever think of going back?"

"No."

"Why not?" she asked, surprised by the vehemence in his voice, the insistence. It made her think he was denying a part of himself, an important part of his life.

He shrugged. "It's over."

"And you like settling down…on a ranch?"

"Never thought of it that way. It's all I know."

She swallowed back any remaining reservations. "I'm sorry for how I sounded earlier. I just meant that—"

"It's okay. Forget it."

How could she? Could she forget that Joe was here, alone, with only the howling wind for company? She fought against taking on this responsibility. It wasn't her concern. But she hadn't been his, either. He'd helped her. And Cody.

She doubted this strong man would appreciate or want help from her. Maybe he didn't think he needed anything or anybody. But everyone needed someone, in some way. Otherwise, loneliness would eat away at him. She didn't want that to happen, but she'd have to tiptoe around his pride.

"Well, I was wondering if you're doing anything tonight." She stalled before taking the plunge. "Cody's been asking about you. Asking when you were coming home. Could you come for dinner tonight?"

* * *

Cody had asked about *his* daddy. Not Joe.

He'd do well to remember that.

But he hadn't. He'd agreed to dinner.

He cautioned himself to remember that Marty had asked him to come. For Cody. Not because she wanted him at her dinner table. She certainly didn't want him to kiss her again. She'd made that abundantly clear.

With a mixture of confusion and anxiety, he sat at the head of the table. The succulent aromas of onions, ham, pinto beans and cornbread filling his head with memories of family and home. He decided at that moment, for this one night, he'd pretend this was his family, just as Cody believed Joe was his father. What harm could it do? Marty certainly didn't have to know.

"How's your head?" he asked, glancing at his "son" sitting on his right.

"Better." Cody stuffed a hunk of ham into his tiny mouth. By his side, Scout sat, woeful eyes staring at the little boy, his tail thumping against the floor.

"Did you feed Scout?" Marty asked.

"Oops." Cody handed the puppy a section of cornbread. In one gulp, Scout swallowed it then licked his lips, hoping for more handouts.

"Cody," Marty admonished. "We don't feed the dog at the table."

"Sorry, Momma." He turned an eager gaze on Joe. "Daddy, can you help me feed him after dinner?"

The sound of "daddy" pinched his conscience, but he ignored it. He wanted to be a daddy. He wanted to father this little boy. He wanted to experience the wonder and excitement of discovering the world through the eyes of a child. For tonight only, he reminded himself. Or until Cody remembered who his real father was. "Sure."

Hooking his spoon into his beans, Cody mumbled, "Scout's always hungry."

"Puppies usually are. And so are growin' boys." Joe ruffled the kid's hair. "Eat up."

"How was your day?" Marty asked, her tone casual as she cut into her slice of ham.

Her simple question startled him. How long had it been since anyone had bothered to ask? His fingers tightened around his fork. "Fine."

A long pause of silence followed. He heard the clink of silverware, Cody's soft chewing, and Scout panting beside him. Feeling as if he'd single-handedly put a halt to the light banter, he remembered his long-lost manners.

"Uh, and you? How was your day?"

Marty gave him a gentle smile, the corners of her eyes crinkling, the brown centers sparkling with golden flecks. "It was good. I work with a resource teacher, and sometimes I get to work one-on-one with the kids, rather than filing or grading or copying papers."

She paused, as if she'd said too much. He nodded and said, "And you got to do that today?"

She plucked at the corner of the place mat. "I worked with this sixth grader. He's really behind grade level. But he tries so hard." She glanced at her son and dropped her voice. "He's had problems at home. Anyway, we read a story together. I asked him questions as we went. And he was able to answer them." She took a sip of her iced tea. "That's a marked improvement for him."

"Sounds like you're a born teacher."

She shrugged, but her cheeks turned bright pink.

"Why don't you teach?" he asked.

She met his gaze squarely, as if confused by his question. "I don't have a degree. I met Flint and…" She fell silent. He read between the lines. She'd met a cowboy, married, had Cody, and never finished school.

"You ought to go back," he said.

She laughed. "In my spare time."

"Someday," he reiterated, his tone serious, "you should get your degree and teach."

"Daddy," Cody said, snagging his attention away from Marty. "How'd you do at the rodeo? Did you win?"

He paused and tried to think of an appropriate answer. The sights and sounds of rodeo, sharp, distinct, exciting, came back full-force. He wasn't exactly truthful with Marty earlier that day. He missed the rodeo more than he wanted to admit. But he would never go back. Finally, glancing away from Cody's eager gaze, he answered, "Not this time."

"Will you stay home for a while now?" Cody asked.

He glanced at Marty for help. Her eyes widened and he read the uncertainty.

"Cody," he started to say, "I, uh—"

"I promise I'll be good." The forlorn voice broke down the last of Joe's barriers.

Stunned by the child's simple promise, Joe felt a heaviness form in the pit of his stomach.

"Cody, baby," Marty said, her voice soft. "Daddy doesn't leave because he thinks you're bad. He has a job to do."

Joe wanted to say something, to help. But what? How could he explain? This was a delicate matter. He could bungle it. Then Marty would kick him out of her house and their lives.

"Look, cowboy." Joe winced at his careless tone. He twirled his fork between his thumb and forefinger, wondering how to broach this topic. "Come here, Cody." Pushing back from the table, he patted his thigh.

Instantly the boy rounded the table and crawled onto Joe's lap. He nestled against his side, warm and trusting as a son should. A fatherly obligation grew inside Joe. His resolve strengthened. He wouldn't let Cody be hurt again. Not if he could help it.

"Cody, my going away...to rodeos...doesn't have anything to do with you. It's what I do. It's how I make a living."

"Like when Momma teaches at school?" Cody asked.

He grinned at his "son" and pushed a shock of the kid's dark hair out of his eyes. "Exactly. In fact, we do these things for you."

Cody's eyes widened.

"So you can stay in this nice house and have food on the table. So your momma can drive her car. Every father has to work. Some go to work during the day. Some work at night. I work mostly weekends at rodeos."

Marty gave Joe a broad smile of appreciation. "That's right, Cody," she added. "You know how your friend Peter's daddy carries a briefcase to work? Well, he works in an office."

"Tommy's dad's a cop." Cody sat up straighter. "He gets to carry a gun, hand out tickets and drive in a real police car."

Marty nodded. "And he works at night, while Tommy's sleeping. When Tommy's at school, his dad's home sleeping."

"And my daddy rides bulls and broncs." He hooked his arm around Joe's neck. "Cool."

Joe chuckled and exchanged a warm smile with Marty. Maybe this parenting thing wasn't so tough. "Someday you'll have your own job. You'll have to go to work and earn a living to provide for your family. You said you wanted to be a cowboy. If you do get the chance, then you'll have to travel around the country and go to different rodeos. Like...me."

He noticed a slight frown creasing Marty's brow. Had he gone too far? Should he not have given Cody the idea of traveling in his father's—real or imagined—footsteps?

"Then you're not mad at me?" Cody asked, his voice shy, his head leaning against Joe's shoulder.

His throat convulsed at the relief in the boy's voice. His anger focused on Flint Thomas. What kind of a father was he? What had he said to make Cody feel responsible? Joe's conscience tapped him on the shoulder and reminded him that if his child had lived, he might have been as bad a father. If not worse. "I'm not mad at you, Cody."

He wanted to say more. Cody needed reassurance. Joe wanted to tell him that nothing could take him away from his little boy. That he'd always come back. But that would have been a lie. He wished Marty would say something. When he glanced at her for help, he noticed her head was bent forward. She sniffed quietly.

Joe knew she blamed herself for Cody's problem with the divorce. But he blamed Flint. His chest swelled with anger.

Cody hugged him tight. Over his tangle of brown hair, Joe met Marty's watery gaze. Her mouth moved and he read her lips. *Thank you.* Something inside him softened. A rush of heat pumped through his veins.

When Cody pulled back, he grinned. His eyes lit up like a clear night sky. "Can you teach me to ride?"

"Well, uh, I guess I can." His gaze lifted to Marty's once again. Her eyes were wide, her body stiff. Great. He'd done it again. Now she'd have his head. "We'll have to wait," he added, "until the doctor says it's okay and your mom agrees."

Cody turned around. "Can we, Momma? Can Daddy teach me to ride?"

"Not for a while," she said, her voice sounding like brittle branches breaking. "Finish your dinner, baby." Her gaze locked with Joe's. This time he read something completely different. He knew once more he'd crossed an invisible line.

When would he learn?

Chapter Five

"No more stories," Marty said with a tired smile, closing the cowboy book and placing it on the bedside table.

Cody gave her frown. "But, Momma—"

"No more water, either. You've had enough to float a ship." She ruffled his hair, and he scrunched down beneath the covers.

She felt Joe's gaze on her as he stood at the end of the bed, watching, noticing, distant yet a part of their nighttime ritual, and she glanced at him. He held on to Scout's collar while the puppy's tail twitched with excitement. In his other hand, Joe held a Winnie-the-Pooh cup, and the contrast between his dark, roughened fingers and the smooth, plastic child's cup made Marty smile.

Somehow she'd expected the evening to be awkward, but it hadn't. Having Joe in their home somehow felt right. Her son had smiled; his high-pitched laughter something she hadn't heard much of since the divorce. It had given Marty a warm feeling of gratitude toward Joe. He'd said the right things to try to ease her son's burden. Joe seemed to mesh in a natural way with her little family.

He wasn't a stranger anymore. A small crisis had formed a tiny, fragile bond of friendship between them, holding them all together in a delicate situation. His care and concern for her child had wiped away her wariness. Or most of it. Cody had worn down Joe's hardened, crusty exterior to reveal a soft, tenderness in his heart. He seemed lonely, deserted. That had ripped away her barriers. She cared about this cowboy. Far more than she should.

But she only offered friendship, she reminded herself. It was the least she could do after all he'd done for her and Cody.

With a sigh, she kissed the top of her son's head, touched his cheek and whispered, "I love you." Straightening from the bed, she said, "Now get some sleep, Cody. You have school tomorrow."

He nodded then reached out his hands for Joe. "Daddy?"

Joe stiffened, his knuckles turning white against the yellow cup. He glanced at Marty, uncertainty clouding his dark blue eyes. She stepped back and nodded her okay for him to give her son a hug and kiss good-night. With hesitant steps, he moved past her.

His arm brushed her shoulder. She glanced up, noticing his height, his strength, the power in the coiled muscles that he controlled with an economy of motion. Beneath his rugged exterior, she glimpsed a subtle anxiety tightening his features. It made him seem less rough-and-tough cowboy and far more sexy.

Her nerves snapped in two. Cowboys weren't sexy. They were trouble. She would do well to remember that.

Watching this seasoned cowboy treat her son with infinite care, giving him a tender kiss and gentle hug, Marty felt her heart contract. Cody wrapped his arms around Joe's neck and smacked a kiss onto his cheek.

"Are you gonna fix me breakfast tomorrow?" Cody asked, his wide, innocent eyes looking up at his "father."

Joe coughed and sat on the bed. His larger frame dented the mattress, making the little boy shift toward him. "Well, Cody, I've got to go to work early. I don't think you'll be up by the time I leave."

Marty nodded her approval of his excuse.

Cody's bottom lip protruded. "Another rodeo?"

"No," Joe answered. "I promised to help a friend work his cattle. But don't you worry, I'll be back in time for supper. Okay?"

Slowly, Cody nodded. "Can we have pizza?"

"You'll have to ask your mother about that," he said with a soft chuckle.

"Momma?"

"We'll see." She tapped Joe on the shoulder, indicating it was time to leave. As they walked out the bedroom door, they paused. In unison, they turned and reached for the light switch. Their hands touched. Joe caught her fingers against his warm palm. He tossed a smile in her direction and flipped the switch. But an electrical current pulsed through her.

"Good night, cowboy," Joe said over his shoulder. His voice melted over her like fine chocolate on her tongue.

She knew then she'd started to think of Joe in a way that was far too dangerous. Could he become Cody's father? It was too tempting to let him step into that role, erase Flint's memory, heal her son's broken heart. What would he be like as a husband? Could he make her feel again, awaken her to the passions and desires she'd long forgotten?

The questions made her head spin, her heart pound, her knees weaken. Hope, frightening and dangerous as it was, sprang within her. Terrifying her. Because she knew the raw pain of disappointment.

* * *

"You promised you'd teach him to ride," Marty said. It was not a question. Her voice sounded flat with an underlying waver that warned Joe of her building fury. He'd seen the quick flashes flare at his blunders with Cody. He fully expected this one.

They'd moved from Cody's room back to the kitchen. The intimacy of the tucking-in-bed ritual clung to him like a sweet, bitter scent. It had shaken Joe to his very core. Cody's trusting embrace, Marty's soothing voice, had made him long for something he didn't deserve. The more time he spent with them, the more he realized what he'd lost. The deprivation made his insides tremble. His heart ached with a dull thud against his breastbone. A part of him wanted desperately to be a part of this family. Was that wish only a means of replacing all he'd lost? It didn't matter. He knew the impossibility of it ever happening.

He stared out the kitchen window into the darkness beyond. Tiny lights twinkled in the velvety night sky. He felt as distant from hope as he did from those stars.

He only knew that if he was going to play daddy, then he was going to do it right. This time.

Responding to Marty's statement, he faced her then, his determination full of conviction. "I did promise Cody I'd teach him to ride. And I'm not sorry about it."

She stared at the sink, her hands hidden in soapy water. Her profile looked stark, her skin pale. The corner of her mouth drew down in a frown. She opened it but promptly shut it without commenting.

Jamming his hands into his jeans' pockets, Joe hunched his shoulders against the weight of her anger as if preparing for a confrontation with a blustering wind. "I know you're gonna blame me for—"

"I'm not blaming you." The stillness of her voice stopped him.

His nerves set on edge, he lifted his head and stared at

her, watching her slow, precise movements. She pulled her hands out of the water, which lapped against the sides of the sink. Slowly she dried them on a towel, folded it and laid it on the counter. She had soft, slender hands that could be tough and defensive, or comforting and gentle. But he remembered her hand tentatively resting against his chest when he'd kissed her, hovering between the automatic urge to push him away and the sensual need to pull him closer. He wanted to feel her hands on him once more. Shrugging off that thought, he knew she wouldn't allow him that close ever again.

Without looking at him, she plucked at the tiny fringed edge of the towel with her fingertips. "I'm stunned, is all. You've done so much for us—for Cody. I guess I have a hard time accepting that you'd want to do more. I feel..." She glanced at him then, her brown eyes round with uncertainty. "It's overwhelming."

"You're not mad?"

She shook her head and sniffed. "No. In fact, I'm moved."

He arched his eyebrows in surprise. He'd expected anger, fear, a mother lion's defense of her child. But he hadn't expected this. The tender vulnerability in her eyes tugged him toward her. Using what little common sense he had left, he resisted pulling her into his arms. He prayed she wouldn't cry. He couldn't handle it if she did.

Sensing something else, something she held back, an ubiquitous "but," he braced himself for more. "You don't exactly seem happy about my offer, though."

"No." She brushed her hair back from her face, hooking the thick, mahogany locks behind her ears. "I don't know how to react. I keep thinking you're leaving, and you find another reason to stay. It doesn't make sense to me. Why would you want to help my son? Cody cares about you. But when does all this end? And how will I mop up my son's tears?''

He sucked in a breath that burned his tight lungs. He didn't have answers to her questions. But he knew it all would end. Probably the sooner the better.

How could he explain his need to help Cody? Fact was, it didn't stop with the child. His need grew stronger when he looked at Marty. He didn't understand it himself. Or maybe he did. But he didn't want to face it or explain anymore. He'd never spoken to anyone about his family, his mistakes. He didn't see the purpose now.

Shrugging, he said, ''Your son is hard to say no to.''

She rubbed her eyes and looked at him with deep sorrow. ''Strange, his real father doesn't seem to have a problem with that. Flint's always finding excuses. Well, at first he says yes or offers to do something special with Cody, then he *always* backs out of his promise.''

Joe ducked his head and studied the tips of his boots. The kid's pain was like a raw nerve in Joe's gut. Every time he saw those brown eyes, which reminded him so much of Marty, he wanted to track down Flint and punch the guy out. ''I know.''

''What you said earlier at dinner to Cody was really sweet.'' She took a step toward him. ''I think it helped.''

Her dark, hooded gaze made him think she was holding more back. ''But?''

She sighed, swelling her chest and pushing the air through her pursed lips. ''They're just words. He's young, but he knows the difference between honest actions and empty promises. He knows more than a job is keeping his father away. He can read through Flint's pitiful excuses like a superhero with X-ray vision. Flint rarely, if ever, calls. He never lives up to his promises. He probably won't even come for Cody's birthday party, much less call or remember it.

"Oh, I'll remind him." She rubbed her palms down the tops of her jean-clad thighs. "I want Flint to look good in his son's eyes. For Cody's sake. But Flint will forget. He always does." She placed a tentative hand on Joe's arm. Her fingers felt warm and moist, soft as satin and delicate as a dewy rose. His gut clenched with something akin to need.

"You've shown my son what a father should be. You've made him happy, made him feel loved and accepted. For that, I'm grateful." Her voice cracked.

Joe took a step away from her, breaking contact, needing extra breathing room. He felt the weight of Flint's mistakes on his own shoulders. He felt the burden of his own inadequacies burn in his gut like a raging fire. Marty shouldn't make him out to be better than Flint. If she only knew the truth.

Shrugging his shoulders, he said, "Right now Cody thinks I'm his father. So it's given him hope. He's probably confused by the past, his memory loss, and how I'm treating him. He wants to believe in his daddy."

"He feels responsible for our divorce." She clasped her hands together, twisting her fingers like a dishrag. "You heard him at dinner. He's scared his daddy's mad at him. He's scared he did something bad that made Flint go away.

"I've tried over and over to explain it to him. But he's awfully young to understand the intricacies of marriage and all the things that can go wrong. He's taken our divorce really hard."

Joe nodded, feeling the tightness in his chest pinch his heart with the innocent questions Cody had asked during dinner. "And Flint? Has he tried to talk to his son about it?"

"No. He won't listen long enough for me to explain. He thinks Cody will get over it. Like he has the mumps or something. Like we both got over our marriage." She bent her head and brushed away a tear. "I feel so help-less." Her voice wobbled. "I can't help my son. I can't give him what he really needs."

Joe wanted to enfold her in his arms, hold her, give her a shoulder to cry on, take away her pain. But he wouldn't make that step. That mistake. "What do you think he needs?"

"A male influence. A real dad." She blew a breath out between her lips and stared up at the ceiling as if for an-swers.

She was right.

Cody needed a dad.

Marty needed a husband.

But Joe wasn't volunteering. He couldn't be a good fa-ther. He couldn't be a good husband, either. Even if Marty wanted him, which he doubted. Still, he had to do what he could until some better man came along. No matter how much it tortured him.

"The funny thing is…" Marty continued with a bitter laugh, "and it's really not so funny, it's tragic… You're more real to Cody as a dad than his biological father ever was."

Abruptly, she turned, faced the sink and twisted on the tap water. She grabbed plate after plate off the counter, scraped away the leftover food, then placed them in the dishwasher. After a long pause, she said in a voice as tight as he felt inside, "I just don't know what to do for Cody anymore."

In that instant Joe knew he'd say something he'd prom-ised never to discuss. This wasn't to relieve his conscience or to make himself feel any better. He was doing this for Marty.

Feeling his throat constrict with rough emotions, he coughed. This had to be done. She needed the understanding more than he needed to avoid the pain. But he'd only tell her so much.

Taking her small shoulders between his hands, he turned her toward him.

Startled by his touch, his closeness, the intensity of his gaze, Marty stared up at him. The lines on his face seemed deeper. The burning pain in the depths of his blue eyes flared like a laser to pierce her with a searing heat.

His mouth twisted. "Marty," he said, his voice thick. "I know what you're going through. The helplessness. The pain. Sometimes there's nothing you can do but love the one you're trying to protect. You can't always make things better for them. Just being there for Cody is more important than any words you could ever say."

She felt the muscles along her throat tense, convulse with a suppressed sob. How long had it been since she'd opened up to someone, shared her inability to be supermom, admitted any weakness? Relief overwhelmed her, gratitude stole part of her control. She wanted more than anything to lean into Joe, absorb his strength, feel his calm, understanding heartbeat beneath her cheek.

But that would be foolish. Hadn't she learned her lesson with his goodbye kiss? She trembled beneath his solid grip on her arms.

"Like you said, Cody knows the difference between empty words and honest actions. He might think you're just trying to make him feel better. Over time, as he matures, he'll come to understand all of this."

"How…" she sputtered, her voice weak. She swallowed and tried again. "How'd you get to be so wise, Joe?"

He shook his head. "I'm the furthest thing from that. I'm probably the most foolish person you will ever meet. I was—am like Flint."

He turned away from her, his shoulders drooping forward in fatigue, or pain, or guilt. She didn't know which. Goose bumps rose on her arms where his hands had pressed against her flesh. Compelled, she followed after him. He stopped near the bay window in the breakfast nook overlooking the redwood deck. She watched his set face, his clamped mouth, his fixed gaze reflected in the window. A muscle flexed along his jaw. The tension she sensed inside him made the air around them pulsate.

Without thinking of the consequences, she placed her hand against his back, felt his muscles flinch, a tremor ripple through him. Her own body responded. A tingle shot up her arm. Her insides melted like candle wax beneath a flame.

"I don't believe you. You're not anything like my ex-husband," she said. Joe reminded her of Flint less and less. At first the obvious resemblance of two cowboys had warned her away from him. But in every other way, he'd proven he was responsible, trustworthy, caring. Couldn't he see the differences?

"It's true." His voice sounded gravelly. "I lived for the rodeo. I gave up family and everything normal for my one shot at immortality. How else could I have won three world championships?"

She knew what it took to make it to the top of the rodeo world. She'd seen the toll it had taken on families, friends, her own marriage. Not many made it. Those who did were revered. Those who didn't fell by the wayside, broke, busted and alone. Joe was one of the few who'd gone all the way. He had a different perspective from those that only observed the process.

"Was it worth it?" she asked, fearing she already knew the answer.

"At the time, yes. Now, no."

"It cost you a lot," she said, seeing the pain in his eyes

in the glass reflection, feeling his body harden like concrete beneath her hand.

"It cost me my wife." He shook his head. "And—" His lips compressed into a grim line.

His words resounded in her head as if she'd been slapped against her ear. Her heart galloped in her chest. Her skin burned with sudden realization. Now she knew why his house was empty, devoid of any warmth, filled with dust and cobwebs and a musty odor of neglect. A tender sadness welled up inside her for Joe's heartbreak.

Somehow she understood the pain he suffered. She wanted to smooth away the frown across his forehead. "Did your wife divorce you?"

He shook his head, but didn't speak for a long while. His Adam's apple worked up and down the muscular column of his throat. His tanned skin contracted with each hard swallow, making the hardened veins bulge. He plowed his taut fingers through his hair, leaving tracks in their wake. Sweat dampened the back of his shirt, as if he'd broken a fever.

Troubled by the similarities in their marriages, she pulled her hand away. She'd gotten too close, too personal. Her chest contracted with regret. "I'm sorry, I shouldn't have pried. It's none of my business."

When she started to step away, he grabbed her arm. His fingers dug into her skin, urgent, clutching, desperate. She stared up at his grief-stricken face. Red-rimmed, his blue eyes shone like cobalt. Deep furrows lined his brow and bracketed his mouth. A vein at his temple throbbed.

Before he spoke, she feared his words. Blood roared in her ears, deafening her to everything except what he told her next.

"She died." As quickly as he'd grabbed her, he released her. He stalked into the den, his movements stiff, his head bent, his footsteps hurried.

As if in stunned slow motion, she trailed after him, wanting to speak. But her heart lodged in her throat. Tears stung her eyes at the pain registering on this man. Sometime between her fight for independence and his insistence on helping her and Cody, she had begun to care for Joe. She'd started to dig beneath the hardened outer shell and realize he wasn't the typical cowboy she'd grown to despise and disrespect.

"What happened?" she asked, afraid to hear more yet desperate to know what haunted him. She felt closer to Joe than she had ever felt toward Flint. She felt his raw aching pain as if it were throbbing with the beat of her own heart.

He took an unsteady breath. "It was a car accident. Five years ago."

The silence between them electrified. His tortured gaze stole her breath. He wiped a tear from her cheek. She licked at the salty wetness on her lips.

"Don't cry for me," he said. "It was my fault."

"What?" The word rushed out of her before she could catch it on her tongue. "How?"

A sorrow so deep and unimaginable filled his eyes that she could only guess at the depth. She knew from his pinched expression that he cursed himself. Punished himself.

Staring out the window into the dark, forbidding yard, he said, "Because I was a damn fool. Because I failed them. Because I wasn't there."

He'd said too much.

Behind him, he heard Marty fighting back tears, sniffling as she wrestled with a tissue. He hadn't wanted her pity. He'd wanted to help her. But had his confession only made it worse?

He wished he could take back everything he'd said. He

hadn't meant to go so far. He had to backtrack, to explain how all this correlated with her suffering for Cody's sake.

"When Samantha, my wife, was lying in that hospital bed," he said, blocking out his own pain and concentrating on helping Marty, "with all those tubes and wires stuck to her, I felt totally helpless. There was nothing I could do but listen to that damn blip-blip-blip of the heart machine, watch her chest rise and fall with the movement of the respirator."

He shook his head, remembering the smell of antiseptic, the pale gray pallor of his wife's face, the gentle touch of a nurse's hand on his shoulder as he'd clung to his wife's hand. Over the years he'd blocked the images out of his mind, buried his reaction. Now they confronted him full-force, made his stomach churn and bile rise in his throat. He swallowed hard.

"I'd thought I was strong, invincible. Hell, I'd ridden bulls and broncs like there was no tomorrow. I'd ridden into hell and back. But nothing—no injury, no loss—had ever zapped me like this did. It brought me to my knees. I was useless...worthless. I couldn't do anything to help her."

Slowly he looked at her, hoping to see understanding rather than horror in her eyes. He could curse himself. God could sentence him to damnation. But he didn't think he'd survive if Marty's gaze held any accusations.

Her eyes brimmed with tears that streaked her face. What he saw in those depths was like a solid punch to his gut. His breath left him. His heart stopped for a beat, maybe two. When she reached for him, he thought he might break down once more.

But he'd promised himself he wouldn't. Not since Samantha's death. He'd stored his emotions in a dark, hidden place until he felt as if he'd run out of room, until they seeped through the cracks.

Taking a step back, not allowing her to touch him, he squared his shoulders. He had to turn this conversation away from him, away from the pain inside him. He had to get his thoughts and feelings back under tight-reined control. "You feel responsible for Cody. Like I did for my...wife. You're in charge of raising him on your own. But you can't protect him from everything. That's impossible."

"You weren't responsible for the accident. Not if you weren't there," she said adamantly.

He shrugged, knowing full well that he bore the weight of guilt. Marty didn't know everything that he'd lost, what his drive had cost him. "When my wife was in that coma, I realized I hadn't loved her enough. Not like she'd deserved. But I had those last few days to stand by her side, hold her hand, weep for everything she'd lost.

"I never cried for me. I didn't deserve tears. But she did."

His son did.

"Oh, Joe, I'm so sorry," she said. "How did you survive all of that?"

"I did what I had to do." He watched moths flutter around the porch light, dancing near the flame, testing their boundaries, their safety limits. How long had he done that? Until his luck burned up in a single fiery accident.

Inside, he shivered at the cold chill enveloping his soul. The frigid nothingness felt better than the hot emotions ready to burst out of him.

A warm, solid touch jolted him out of his introspection. He glanced first at Marty's delicate hand resting on his shoulder then at her upturned face. Her skin glistened with tears. He didn't want her tears, but somehow they softened a part of his heart. With the roughened pad of his finger, he wiped her cheeks, the corner of her mouth, the curve along the bottom of her lip.

His skin tingled with heat. His breath caught in his chest. Somehow, from Marty, these salty, sweet tears felt cleansing. Maybe she could cry for him, because he'd lost the ability.

She tilted her face into his hand and wrapped her fingers around his wrist. "Thank you for telling me. Thank you for..."

He cupped her jaw in the palm of his hand, smoothed his thumb along the straight, proud line and down the supple column of her throat. In that moment he realized he needed Marty, needed her like food, water and air. He tilted his head and tested her mouth with his.

The seam of her lips parted, and a sigh escaped like a whispered plea. He took in her breath, savored it like a sweet memory. His heartbeat quickened. Blood rushed through his veins. Eagerness surged within him. But he waited. And watched. His gaze locked on hers, looking for resistance, hesitation, reluctance. But she lifted her face more fully, giving him free access. His heart turned over.

Slowly, as if they had all the time in the world, as if this kiss had to last forever, he covered her mouth with his. Their lips merged. Their breaths mingled. Their mouths meshed into one.

Mindlessly craving the sweet taste of her, he devoured her mouth. Heat suffused his body. Her sensually soft fragrance aroused his senses. Each labored breath sounded ragged in his ears. Each touch felt softer, more urgent. She pressed her warm, lithe body against his, chests meeting, bellies touching, hips aligning. Wild, hot sensations numbed his mind to any rational thought. Questions and common sense crumbled beneath the onslaught of desire.

He moved his hands over her, settling against the small of her back, molding her against him. He kissed her mouth, her chin. She tasted salty and sweet. Nibbling his way to her earlobe, he felt her shiver in his arms. A seductive moan rose in her throat and echoed in his mind.

"Oh, Joe." Her hands clasped his shoulders.

Shaken by his need, petrified of hers, he stopped, pulling away. He sucked in a sharp, inadequate breath.

"W-what did you do that for?" she asked, her brown eyes cloudy and dark.

"What do you mean? Why'd I kiss you? Or why'd I stop?"

She touched her fingertips to her mouth. Her eyes were wide, but he couldn't read the emotion churning in those dark depths. After a long awkward moment, she said, "The kiss. You shouldn't have—"

"Don't blame it on me." He had no room for any more guilt. But he also knew he shouldn't have kissed her, shouldn't want her so damn much, shouldn't need her with every fiber. "You wanted it. I wouldn't ever do anything that wasn't mutual between us."

She met his gaze. He recognized that flare of anger. But she didn't speak, didn't deny it. For that he was grateful.

"Look, Joe," she said, her voice shaky, her hands trembling. "Maybe you should just go."

Her words cut through his defenses, but he clenched his teeth and bit down on his disappointment.

She shrugged, settling her shoulders in firm resolve. "I mean, Cody's gone to sleep. He doesn't usually wake up in the night." Her voice grew stronger. "I appreciate what you're doing for him. But let's keep it between you two. You and I don't need to get involved. Okay?"

His gaze narrowed on her meaning. "You mean, you don't want to get involved. With me."

"With anyone."

"With another cowboy." Understanding clanged in his mind like cymbals. It was time to go. He wouldn't stay where he wasn't wanted...or needed. A knife of truth twisted in his gut. He wasn't needed. By Cody. Or especially by Marty. Why that should hurt him, he didn't know. He didn't want to know. He turned to leave.

"Joe."

Reluctantly he glanced back at her.

"It's not you. I don't mean this personally." She clasped her arms across her stomach. "It's just that…well, you may have to pretend you're Cody's father, but you and I don't have to pretend we're married."

"I wasn't pretending." The coldness in his voice made her flinch. He hadn't pretended to care for her or to want her. He had. He did. As he hadn't wanted or cared for anyone in years. Maybe that was his sin.

He walked out her door. This time, the emptiness in his heart was like a vacuum. It swallowed him whole.

Chapter Six

A gentle ripple of laughter stirred Marty from a deep sleep. She stretched her tired muscles and shifted onto her side. Her thoughts drifted like cobwebs in a breeze. From outside, she heard Scout's whine and bark. With her heart kicking into full gear, she placed her bare feet on the nubby carpet, then remembered it was Saturday.

Flopping back onto the bed, she enjoyed a few minutes of quiet. All to herself. It had been a long week of scurrying around, taking Cody to and from school, working in between as the teacher's aide, grocery shopping, washing clothes, ironing, straightening the house. She didn't even have time to think how she'd ever squeeze in the last of her college courses to become a full-fledged teacher. Sometimes, she felt like a gerbil running on a wire wheel, getting nowhere fast. At least she didn't have to mow the lawn in January.

In the middle of the week she'd taken Cody back to the doctor. "Be patient," the doctor had said. "He's fine."

Yes, her son was fine. Except he couldn't remember his *real* father.

Each night for the past week she'd cooked dinner for Cody and Joe. He'd come over in late afternoon, pretend they were a happy family and leave after tucking her son in bed. It was a farce, and it grated on her. She hated lying to her son, encouraging his fantasy. Worse, she felt indebted to Joe. But each time he arrived at their house, relief swept over her.

Her nerves had been on edge since that passionate kiss that had set her senses on fire. Why had he stopped? She hadn't been able to find the strength to resist him. She knew she'd wanted more. But when he'd pulled back, she'd felt a wave of embarrassment crash over her. He hadn't rejected her with words. But his look, the simple act of pushing away from her, had crushed her. She'd wanted to pretend his kiss meant nothing.

Brushing back her hair with her fingers, she sat on the edge of the bed and stared at herself in the mirror. For more than a year she'd lived with her husband's rejection. Oh, Flint hadn't turned her away. But he hadn't turned away other women, either. It made her feel inadequate, homely, unappealing. Did Joe see her as just a mom? He hadn't mentioned their kiss again. Surreptitious glances had passed between them this past week. They'd gone out of their way to avoid touching, brushing shoulders, grazing fingertips. Her stomach felt as if it had been tied in the perfect Boy Scout knot.

When Joe arrived each evening, her heartbeat had accelerated. She'd started taking more care with her hair and makeup. Most of the time she never bothered with lipstick. But lately she'd started applying it daily. She didn't want to look like a mom. She wanted to be seen as a woman. But that was foolish. Catching Joe's attention was a waste of time and energy.

Her chest tightened at the memory of Joe telling her about his wife. She ached for him. It had been a natural reaction. What worried her was that jealousy had reared up inside her. How she longed for a man to love and cherish her as Joe did his dead wife. Shamed by that silent admission, she knew she couldn't compete with a memory, any more than she'd been able to compete with the other women in Flint's life.

Nothing made sense anymore. Her nerves were frayed, her emotions twisted and rolled up like a ball of yarn batted back and forth between a pair of kitten's paws. She didn't know what she wanted, what she needed. She even doubted what she knew was best for Cody.

Another bark, followed by a squealing giggle, caught her attention. The commotion sounded like it came from outside. She squinted at the light seeping through the miniblinds that made long shadows across the peach carpet. Moving to the window, she separated two slats and peered out into the early morning brightness.

Sunlight bathed the backyard in a swath of shimmering gold, making the dew sparkle like tiny diamonds. The lanky black Lab bounded over the two-foot-high brick wall surrounding the patio and skirted across the faded grass. He pounced on the bright red ball, clamped it between his jowls, then faced the house, wagging his tail with pride.

"Scout!" Cody called from the patio. "Bring it here, boy. Bring it here."

Marty smiled and leaned against the wall, enjoying the lazy morning. Only in the past week had Cody started to smile again. Since the divorce he'd withdrawn from her happy-go-lucky little boy to a sad, inhibited child. What had lifted his spirits?

Joe.

He'd had a powerful effect on her child. He'd shown Cody how a responsible man should act, how a father should treat his son. He'd given Cody a family, even if it was a charade.

He'd changed her, too. Although, she hated to admit it. She'd grown used to his smile, his advice, his being there.

But he couldn't always be with them. This had to end sometime, she reminded herself. But how? When? And what price would they all pay when it was over?

She watched the dog shake his head, toss the ball in the air and pounce on it. Like a shot of aged-in-the-keg whiskey, a low, rumbling laugh reached Marty. She knew before he spoke who it was.

"I don't think he's listening, Cody," Joe said, laughter pinching his words.

"What do I do, Daddy?"

"Come on, I'll help."

With her heart pounding in her chest, Marty wondered when he'd arrived this morning. How had he gotten in? She heard the sound of Joe's boots clomp across the wooden deck of the patio. Cody jogged beside him down the three steps. She noticed her son had forgotten his coat, hat and gloves. Wearing a thick flannel shirt and faded jeans, Joe gestured for Cody to move around to the other side of Scout. In her son's eyes, she saw love, respect and awe. Her heart contracted and a lump settled in her throat.

He needed a father.

Joe and Cody separated then converged on the frisky puppy. Cody made the overt attack, lunging with his arms outstretched. Scout yelped and dodged back, knocking into Joe's legs. Together, all three tumbled to the ground in a tangle of arms, legs and playful yips.

Laughing, Joe rolled onto his back. His Stetson fell off his head, revealing his tousled hair, which grazed his collar. Cody collapsed across his stomach, his cries of glee rebounding throughout the neighborhood. Scout pounced on them, licking at their faces with his pink tongue.

A chuckle escaped Marty's lips and startled her. Her smile faded for a moment before she gave in to the giddy feeling and enjoyed a full, relaxing grin. This is what Saturday mornings should be like. Why not enjoy having a man around the house? For a change.

She didn't need a man permanently. Only temporarily.

"Pizza's here!" Cody ran toward the front door.

Joe smiled and followed, beating Marty to the door. With a smug glance in her direction, he handed the delivery boy a ten-dollar bill and took the warm box. As with the other pizza nights over the past three weeks, a cheesy, spicy aroma filled the house.

They'd set this pattern that first weekend he'd spent here. Of course, he hadn't stayed the night. He still didn't. But when he slept at home, he dreamed of holding Marty. He usually left as soon as Cody went to bed, drove the twenty minutes to his ranch then returned early the next morning after he'd fed cattle so his "son" wouldn't discover anything amiss.

"You didn't have to do that," Marty whispered when Cody had bounded into the other room to grab his plate, a playful Scout at his heels. She held out a ten-dollar bill to replace the one he'd spent on them. "Here take this."

"No," Joe answered. He gave her a wink. "It was my pleasure."

The stern set of her jaw told him she wasn't thrilled with his generosity, but she covered her irritation with a reluctant, "Thanks." She met his gaze squarely. It made his gut tighten, since most of the time these days they never stared directly at each other. "You've done so much for us already. You don't have to pay for our dinner, too."

He placed a hand on her arm, keeping her from escaping into the kitchen, into Cody's safer proximity. "I don't mind. This isn't a hardship for me. I enjoy your—er, Cody's company."

She glanced down at his hand, his tanned fingers curling

over her forearm. Instead of reprimanding him for crossing the invisible fortress she'd built between them, she said, "I know."

His heart stilled for a brief pause. He wanted to press her for more of an answer. Did she understand his loneliness? Did she feel the same as he did? Did she enjoy his company, too?

Pulling his hand away, he stuck his thumb through a belt loop and shook his head. She made her way to Cody's side, helping her son carry his plate and drink to the table. He shouldn't be having thoughts like that. She'd told him flat-out she wasn't interested in pursuing anything between them. When Cody's memory came back, Joe would be out the door faster than a rowdy drunk booted out of a Dallas honky-tonk.

Part of him wished the kid's memory would come back fast. The longer they dragged this out, the harder it was going to be. For Joe. But another part of him wanted to play Cody's father forever. That made him sweat.

After finishing off the cheesy pizza, Cody showed his "parents" where they should sit on the sofa. Joe guessed he was much too close to Marty, because she shifted, crossing her legs away from him, putting a little more space between them. Beneath the soft veil of her shoulder-length black hair, the top of her cheeks brightened to a rosy hue. Cody wiggled between them and waited for the start of the video he'd selected. Joe glanced over the kid's disheveled hair at Marty. Her gaze locked with his. Briefly. Those eyes darkened to almost black, as if worry churned in their depths.

"You okay?" Joe mouthed before she glanced away. As she always did.

She gave a quick shake of the head, indicating nothing, and turned her attention back to the television and the lanky cowboy preparing to ride a bull.

"I'm gonna ride one of those someday," Cody said, "just like my daddy." His hand settled on Joe's knee.

The innocent comment was like a sharp rowel raking down Joe's spine. His fist contracted. For the first time Joe realized his view of rodeo had changed, from something he'd *decided* not to do, to something he no longer *wanted* to do. When Samantha died, he'd forced himself to retire, but he'd battled the need to return to the circuit for five years. Had he lost the urge for that heart-stopping excitement? He'd punished himself by staying away. But when had the drive died? What had changed his heart? Cody? Marty? He wasn't sure he wanted an answer to his troubling questions.

He wished he didn't have to pretend to rodeo anymore. He hated the idea that Cody believed he was Flint—with rodeo as his first priority, instead of family. For some reason Joe wanted to prove he wasn't like Cody's real dad, he wasn't the way he used to be.

As the movie progressed, so did the romantic interest between the two lead actors. Cody grew restless. He finally settled against Joe's side, warm and trusting, and Joe slipped an arm around him.

"Is he asleep?" Marty whispered, nodding toward her son a while later.

"Nope." Cody struggled to sit up, rubbing his eyes and stretching his arms wide. "I don't like the kissin' parts."

Joe laughed. "You will, cowboy." He cut his eyes toward Marty. "Someday you will."

She flushed and pushed up fast from the couch as if she'd received an electric shock from the cushion. "Anybody want some popcorn?"

"Yeah!" The last traces of sleep disappeared from Cody's smiling eyes. He gave the television one last glance, his gaze caught by the sight of a cowboy being tossed from a bull.

Joe stiffened. He'd seen cowboys take worse hits in a rodeo. When it took place right in front of you, it reminded you of your own mortality. Something cowboys rarely liked to face.

"It's okay," Cody said, having seen this movie a dozen times. "He's not hurt." As the cowboy on the screen stood and dusted himself off, Cody focused on Joe. The little boy's gaze widened, his hand tightening on Joe's thigh. "That won't happen to you, Daddy." His voice wavered. "You won't get hurt, will you?"

The plea in Cody's voice ripped through him. His throat tightened. He hugged the boy close, his hand patting Cody's back. "No, son. I'll be careful."

That he could guarantee. He didn't ride anymore. But he couldn't promise it wouldn't happen to Flint. Guilt twisted his heart for not being able to protect this good kid from his own father's stupidity. Was that why the desire to rodeo had vanished? Had he started to care about Cody and Marty too much? A pain sliced through him. He'd never worried about his mortality while married, not even when Samantha had been carrying his son. Did that mean he hadn't loved his wife enough...or his son? Guilt tightened its screws into Joe's heart.

"Come on, Cody," she said, loosening her son's grip on Joe. "Help me make some popcorn. Then it'll be time for bed."

Joe stayed in the den, hearing the rustle of paper, then the slow pop of kernels in the microwave. He knew it was almost time for him to head on home. Like he did every night. But he wished he could stay...forever.

Which raised another question, one more devastating. If his original punishment, the one he'd set for not being there for Samantha and his son, no longer caused him pain, then how would he punish himself now? By taking away what he wanted more than anything—another chance. One with Marty and Cody.

"What's wrong?" Joe asked as he headed toward the door. With Cody tucked in bed, there was no reason to stay. But he found himself lingering, reluctant to leave.

Their home had begun to feel more like his than his own. He found himself dreading having to go back to his ranch and, more and more, looking forward to his return. *This isn't your home, Joe. This isn't your family. Go home, where you belong.* He once again reminded himself that he wasn't Cody's dad or even Marty's husband. He wouldn't ever be. That was impossible. The idea of accepting responsibility for them rattled his nerves and shook his confidence. What if he were to fail again? He couldn't live with that. He wouldn't risk making another fatal mistake. But he couldn't turn his back on them, either.

"Oh, I'm all right." She arched her back. "I guess I'm just tired."

"Need a back rub?" he asked, knowing her answer before she spoke. When her startled gaze met his, he smiled. "You seem a little out of sorts this evening," he said, hoping she'd confide in him.

Her irises contracted to sharp pinpoints of black in a sea of brown despair. "Then your sensors are out of whack. You don't know me very well. I'm usually tired on the weekends."

"You're wrong, Marty." Suddenly he was tired of all the pussyfooting around, dodging each other's glances, ignoring the electricity vibrating between them. He wanted to put his cards on the table. "You don't *want* me to know you. But I do. How could I not, after all this time we've spent together? Fact is, getting close to me scares you."

It sure scared him.

She bristled, squaring her shoulders. "That's just what

a man would think. *You* don't scare me. Whether you know if I'm upset or not, doesn't scare me. The fact that my son still hasn't regained his memory scares me."

She yanked his ego out from under him. He'd been wrong. He'd been wrong about a lot of things. Maybe she wasn't fighting an interest in him. Maybe she was just waiting for the day when he wouldn't have to be a part of their lives. A sharp pain riddled his heart like buckshot. He took a deliberate step back.

"Have you talked to the doctor?" he asked, covering his disappointment with concern.

Marty leaned against the front door with a heavy sigh. "Yeah, he just keeps saying to give Cody time. Give him more time. How much time?"

In her voice, he heard a quiver of panic. "Is there concern that the injury caused…" He paused, unsure how to phrase the delicate question.

"No, his injury healed nicely. There's no permanent damage inside his head. There's no reason he shouldn't remember."

"Maybe there is," Joe said.

She narrowed her gaze on him, her brow furrowing. "You think I should get another opinion?"

He shook his head. "I mean, maybe it's not a head injury. Maybe it's a matter of the heart."

Her eyes widened, then she ducked her head. "I've thought of that. I mentioned it to the doctor. He said if this persists for a few more weeks then he might send Cody to a psychiatrist. What if all this is just an emotional crutch?"

"Then a psychiatrist could help, I guess." He wrestled within himself about whether to offer another solution. One he didn't want to put forth. But it seemed too obvious to ignore. "Have you contacted Flint? Maybe he should come home for a while. I'd, of course, step out of the way." The words tasted bitter in his mouth. He held his breath, waiting for her reply.

"I've tried to call him. I've left messages with several cowboys, but I haven't been able to reach him. He's not good about checking in." She gave a wry laugh. "He wasn't good about that when we were married."

He understood the type. Flint didn't want distractions on the road. Focus on the next rodeo, the next bull. That was the cowboy's credo. Live each moment to its fullest. And they did. The schedule for a rodeo cowboy was grueling, the women abundant, the time scarce. Home and family came a poor second, if not third or fourth.

Joe knew better than anyone the toll it took on a family. He figured Flint didn't much care. The pain and regret in Marty's eyes was evident. But he didn't know how to help her.

"I could call a few friends for you. See if they could help find him," he said.

"That's okay. He'll call when he wants to." For the first time in three weeks she reached out to Joe, placing a tentative hand on his forearm. "If you don't mind, if it's not too much of a hardship on you, I think we have to keep playing along with this until something breaks. I think we're in too deep to back out now."

He knew for certain he was in too deep. And what would break would probably be his heart.

A note of joy whistled through her heart as Marty watched Joe read a Dr. Seuss book to her son. Quiet humor underlined his words. He paused every so often for Cody to fill in the blanks. His exuberance made her eyes swell with grateful tears.

The contrast between the rugged cowboy and her tiny son made Joe look even more imposing, his shoulders broader and thicker, his hands larger, stronger. He had a sturdy, rock-solid quality, not like her ex-husband's lanky, boyish build. This man, holding her son on his lap, was dependable. At the same time, the way Joe turned each yellowed page, chuckled along with her son and swept an errant lock of hair out of Cody's eyes, made him look like the gentlest, most caring soul she'd ever met.

"Another one, Daddy." Cody closed the book with a clap and reached for another on the table beside his bed.

Joe smiled and opened the book. "Don't think I've read this one before."

"It's got a dog that looks sorta like Scout," Cody said. "It don't have many words, just lots of pictures. Momma and me make up the story as we turn the pages."

"I see," Joe said, shifting in the rocking chair and making it squeak.

Marty had been the only person to ever rock Cody in that chair. She remembered the feel of her tiny baby in her arms, snuffling against her shoulder. Flint never had gotten the hang of babies. As he'd said, "He's too fragile. I might break him."

She doubted Joe would be a hands-off daddy. She could easily imagine him changing diapers with infinite care, spooning food into a toddler's mouth, rocking a baby to sleep as it nestled against his broad shoulder.

Whoa, Marty cautioned herself. What was she envisioning? Nothing. Absolutely nothing.

"It's getting late," she said, startling herself out of her delusions. Joe and Cody looked as if they'd been caught with their hand in the cookie jar. "You can read that book next time, Cody."

He frowned. "But, Momma—"

"Tomorrow's a school day, young man. Now, hop into bed."

Scrambling off Joe's lap, Cody crawled into bed, sticking his little feet beneath the covers. "Can I have—"

"A drink of water." Chuckling, Joe stood and walked toward the bathroom. He came back with the familiar yellow cup and handed it to Cody.

"Did you brush your teeth?" Marty asked.

Joe nodded while her son swallowed a gulp. "Already peed, brushed his teeth." He took the empty cup from Cody. "And filled back up again."

She laughed. "Okay. G'night, sweetheart."

"Momma, when can Daddy teach me to ride?"

Marty glanced at Joe, uncertain how to answer, unsure of her feelings. Was she reluctant to put her son in danger? Or was she worried about committing to more time spent with Joe?

She could admit now that she liked Joe, was grateful to him. But how much of his time could she continue to take? How would they ever sever the ties if he continued to play daddy, husband, and caretaker?

"Did you mean, ride a bull or a horse?" Joe asked.

"Both!" Cody's brown eyes gleamed with excitement.

Joe ruffled his hair. "The bull riding lesson will have to wait until you're much older."

"How old?"

"Thirty-five."

"Daddy." Cody frowned. "How long till I can ride a horse?"

Joe glanced back at Marty. She nodded tentatively. She knew she wouldn't be able to put Cody off much longer and she doubted Joe would put her son in danger. She'd leave the decision to Joe. If he wanted to volunteer the time, she'd let him. Obviously, spending time with Joe did Cody a world of good. She couldn't argue with progress. She only had to get her own emotions under control.

"How about next weekend?" Joe offered.

Cody sat up in bed. "Really?"

"Really," Marty said, finding her voice. "Now, you get

some shut-eye. If you stay up too late and make yourself sick, then you won't be able to ride.''

Promptly, Cody flattened his body against the bed and squinched his eyes closed and pretended to softly snore.

Marty's gaze met Joe's, and he gave her a broad wink. He glanced one last time down at his ''son.'' Together, they left the room, Joe switching off the light.

A soft voice reached them at the end of the hall. ''How will I ever sleep between now and then?''

They looked at each other, breaking into wide grins, and laughed at the same time, trying to keep their voices as low as possible. She leaned toward him, breathed in the warm, spicy scent that was distinctly Joe. Her stomach fluttered.

She knew she wasn't just interested in men again. She was interested in this particular man. What she didn't know was what to do about it, how to curb her feelings, or if she should even try.

She wanted a husband. Someone to share her life with. Would Joe be a good candidate? Even if he was a cowboy?

Cody lay in his bed for a long time, his eyes blinking against the darkness. He snuggled down into the warmth of his comforter. Instead of counting sheep, he counted horses. Black ones, red ones, pretty sunny-colored ones. He wanted a horse of his very own someday.

More than that, he wanted a daddy. One who spent all night in the house. One who never went away. One who loved him and Momma more than anything else.

Like changing the channel on the television, his thoughts switched to Joe. He'd make a good daddy. He fixed yummy pancakes and biscuits. He liked to play ball with Scout. He read books, bought pizza, and made up silly knock-knock jokes. Best of all, he kept coming back.

Cody remembered his momma telling him last year

when he blew out his birthday candles to make a wish. When he had his birthday party in two weeks, he'd wish that Joe would marry his momma and become his daddy. Forever.

One day he'd wake up and it would all be real, no more make-believing that Joe lived here, that he loved them, that he belonged to them. He felt bad making Momma worry. But he had to keep pretending. He just had to. He wanted her to be happy, too. Joe could make them both happy. He knew it.

With his thoughts filled with family picnics and riding alongside Joe and Momma on horseback, Cody fell asleep, confident it would all work out the way he wanted it to.

Chapter Seven

Marty watched Joe loop the leather girth through a metal ring and yank it tight with sure, strong, competent hands. The blood-bay gelding tossed an irritated glance over his shoulder and snorted. The snaffle bit jingled. Adjusting the girth, Joe tugged a few more times until the saddle sat squarely on the horse's back.

They stood next to a corral just beyond the shade of the weathered barn. The early Saturday morning sun stole the chill out of the frosty January air, making it the perfect weather for short-sleeved shirts. Above them, the sky looked as blue and clear as Joe's eyes.

Even if she couldn't see them at the moment, with the brim of his Stetson blocking her view and casting a dark shadow over his features, his eyes intrigued and at the same time haunted her. She'd never forget them. Or him. She wasn't sure she wanted to.

He looked rugged and sexy in his pale blue jeans that hugged his slim hips, and soft flannel shirt that sculpted the firm muscles along his back, shoulders and arms. She warned herself to watch her step. She not only had to protect her son from being hurt, but she had to guard her heart.

Her hand cupped the back of Cody's head. Smoothing his silky hair along the nape of his neck, she settled her hand on his tense little shoulder. Fixing a keen, motherly gaze on her son, she watched Cody's eyes widen as Joe mounted the gelding. The leather creaked. The horse shifted. A tiny tremor rippled through Cody.

"Are you cold?" she asked. "Your jacket's in the car."

He shook his head. His gaze remained on the looming horse. Joe heeled his mount and moved past them. The horse's tail twitched, as if he was eager to gallop across the open pasture. Its hooves crunched the sandy soil. After a few paces, with the horse prancing and tossing his head, Joe pulled up on the reins, turned his mount and returned, kicking up a small dust cloud behind them.

Cody edged back, bumping against her legs. She put a steadying hand on his belly. Marty's own stomach muscles clenched. Maybe this hadn't been such a good idea. Maybe they'd rushed Cody. After all, he'd had a frightening fall off of a sheep—a much smaller, less intimidating animal than this restless, stomping giant.

This morning at home he'd seemed eager to ride. He'd pulled on his new black cowboy boots and strapped on his chaps. He looked like a miniature replica of Joe.

The gelding whiffled, the soft sound escaping his thick lips, and shook his head, the bridle and bit jangling. In the distance she heard the lowing of cattle and the squawk of an egret overhead. To show Cody all was safe, she reached out her hand toward the gelding. Its muzzle felt warm and velvety against her palm. Her son moved behind her, peering out from around her hip.

"Good horse," she said in a soothing tone, more for her and Cody's benefit than the horse's.

"His name's Bart," Joe said.

"Come meet Bart, Cody," she offered, stepping away to give her son a chance to edge forward. "Don't you want to pet the horse?"

Cody's large brown eyes dwarfed his pale features. His lips were compressed into a tiny white line.

"Ready, son?" Joe asked, breaking the fragile silence.

Her little boy's gaze remained intent on the huge animal in front of him. Marty shot Joe a worried glance and gave a slight shake of her head. The cowboy's blue eyes softened and warmed her insides.

"Maybe we should try something first," Joe said, pushing the brim of his black Stetson skyward with his thumb. "Why don't I give your momma a ride first?"

Cody stared up at the cowboy, relief and confusion knitting his little brow. "Momma don't like horses."

She felt both of their gazes veer toward her. Cody's expectant, Joe's intense; both were waiting for her to answer.

"It's not that I don't like horses." She simply didn't like the emphasis a cowboy placed on his horse. Cowboys seemed to treat their horses better than wives or girlfriends. Horses, cows and bulls had taken Cody's father away.

Once, a long time ago, she'd enjoyed riding on hot summer days or frosty winter ones when each breath froze like a whispered plea in the morning air. Flint had taken her riding a few times, taught her the basics, talked about bits, bridles and saddles. They'd been in their courtship phase then, when even laundry and yard work would have seemed romantic. She had no time for that sort of nonsense now.

"You like this horse, Momma?" Cody asked, hope lifting his voice.

"Of course, I do." She patted the side of the horse's neck.

"You know how moms are," Joe added. "Always worrying about something."

Cody nodded slowly. He turned a steady gaze on her. The pressure inside her built. She didn't want her son to be afraid, but she wasn't too keen on riding the horse herself.

"She's probably just worried about you riding. She'll see for herself it's safe." Joe urged his mount to sidestep away from them. "Then she won't worry when you ride with me. What do you think?"

Her son gave a jerky nod, then a smile brightened his face.

Sweet gratitude swelled inside Marty's chest. Somehow this man always knew the right thing to say. But his suggestion sent an ice cube of apprehension down her spine. When was the last time she'd ridden?

"You're really going to make me ride?" She lowered her voice so Cody couldn't hear.

"I'm not going to make you do anything you don't want to do," Joe answered, reminding her of what he'd said after their last kiss. An uncomfortable warmth twitched inside her. "It could help your son, though."

She nodded her agreement. If it would help Cody, she'd do anything.

"D'you know how to ride?" he asked.

"It's been a while."

He gave her a light not-to-worry smile. "It's like riding a bike. It'll come back to you. Besides, the horse has the hardest part." He clapped his hand against the side of the gelding's neck in a friendly pat. "And Bart here's got a good, steady gait, a soft mouth and is rarin' to go."

Great, she thought. She tried to grasp a complete thought as they whirled past. What foot went in the stirrup? Which side was she supposed to be on? Wait. Wasn't Joe supposed to dismount first?

She painted on a smile like she would lipstick. "I'll be fine. We'll just take a turn around the pasture there." She maneuvered Cody to the fenced corral. "Stay here, out of the way, sweetheart. I'll be right back."

When she turned back to the horse, Joe was still mounted. Her brow wrinkled. "Okay, I'm ready."

He held out a hand for her to grasp.

She stared at it. "What are you doing?"

"I'm offering you a hand up."

"Shouldn't you get off first?"

His gaze narrowed on hers as he leaned down, making the stirrups creak. "I'm trying to show Cody—" his voice dropped to a whisper "—that there's nothing to worry about when he sits up here with me, safe and secure."

She knew how his arms felt wrapped around her. Safe wasn't how she would describe it. Secure didn't come close. Dangerous seemed more likely. At least for her. She doubted she'd be safe from this cowboy in such close proximity. "You want me to ride double?" Her heart beat its way into her throat. "With you?"

"Don't see anyone else to do the honors." His smile was teasing, the right corner of his mouth curling upward, making the trench along his cheek deepen. "Unless you think it'd be wise to let Cody ride alone."

"Definitely not." She took a deep, steadying breath. "Well, it seems like a good idea."

"Don't be afraid." Barely a whisper, his voice held a husky quality that sent warmth to the pit of her stomach.

She stiffened her spine. "I'm not."

Of you, she thought, or this damn horse. Grabbing his hand, she stuck her foot in the stirrup that he'd vacated. In one swift motion she launched herself toward the saddle. His hands caught her waist and settled her between his rock-hard thighs. His strong arms came around her and nestled her against his firm chest. For one brief moment she felt protected. Then she knew she was in serious trouble.

His scent of spicy aftershave and sun-warmed leather made her senses swirl. Overwhelmed by his raw masculinity that seemed to assault each of her senses, she knew at that moment she wasn't afraid of him. She was afraid of herself...of what could be between them. She put a steadying hand on the saddle horn and prayed this would be a very short ride.

From the moment Marty had settled in the saddle, Joe realized he hadn't thought his plan through. Not clearly, that's for sure. He'd been trying to help Cody, trying to be a good dad. Or had he? Had he only been looking for an excuse to get closer to Marty?

Was he simply acting like a randy bull?

A soft, warm breeze fluttered against his face as the horse began to move beneath them. He breathed in Marty's cozy, clean scent—the floral nuances of her hair and soap along her creamy skin. It made him want to nuzzle her neck and wallow in the fragrance.

Wisps of her fine dark hair tickled the side of his neck. Tortured with the urge to run his fingers through the silky strands, he tightened his grip on the reins. She felt petite, almost tiny, so close to him. The top of her head reached his chin. Her shoulders were narrow, her back straight, her hips flared just slightly, retaining a girlish quality. Her jean-clad bottom fit snugly against him and made his gut clench.

He thought of how a man and woman's body were made to fit closely...intimately together. His thoughts veered toward making love. With Marty. He imagined her body stretched out along his, hot flesh touching sensitized nerve endings. He wanted her. As a man should want a woman.

But he didn't want just sex. He didn't want any woman. He wanted Marty.

He wanted to see her smile at him, a sleepy, contented smile. He wanted to feel her lips against his skin. He wanted her as an integral part of his life.

But was that possible?

In the past few weeks, how easily it had been for him to see himself as a real husband to her. How easily it would be to fall into that trap. But he wasn't husband material any more than he was father material. Even if he was, he didn't deserve even an ounce of happiness. This fairy-tale situation was temporary, he reminded himself for the umpteenth time. Soon they'd move on with their own separate lives.

And he'd remain here. Alone. With only a string of horses and a herd of ornery cattle. And too many regrets.

She shifted, edged forward, then rocked back against him. He grunted, sucking in a breath.

"What's wrong?" She swiveled her shoulders, and her hip pressed hard against him.

"Be still," he cautioned more brusquely than he intended. The saddle he'd chosen was large and accommodating—for one. Two made it more than cozy.

"Oh, I..." Her voice trailed off. Her cheeks reddened. She averted her eyes away from his and shifted back into place. This time, she remained stiff, frozen, as if not daring to move again.

"Are you okay?" Her voice came to him soft on the gentle breeze, warm with a hint of a smile that he only imagined.

"Yeah." A muscle in his jaw flexed.

Frustrated with his own reaction, irritated at feeling as though he were caught in a snare, he heeled Bart. The horse loped across the field, his powerful muscles lunging and thrusting them forward. Marty fell back against Joe, startled by the sudden motion. His arm caught her to him, held her there against him. Her hand grabbed his thigh, and shock waves rolled through his body.

Then her body began to move with the horse...and him. She leaned into the wind. He knew her body remembered the motions, the easy feel of a good horse. Sometimes when Joe rode alone, he wished he could run hard and fast, not stopping until he was far away from Marty and her son. But something, his sense of duty, his heart—or more likely his stupidity—kept bringing him right back, continued to torture him, began to break his heart.

He'd been right, the horse's gait was smooth, but the fast rocking motion did little to relieve the tension building inside his body. It wasn't the ride, he knew. It was Marty. Being near her was like being an alcoholic working in a bar, never able to indulge and forever tempted.

After only fifty yards or so, he turned Bart back toward the barn and slowed him to a clipped walk. When they reached the corral where Cody waited, Joe pulled back on the reins. Bart came to a reluctant stop. The little boy grinned and clapped his hands. Neither Joe nor Marty responded.

He stuck his elbow out, and she looped her arm through it. She swung down from the horse as if they'd done the maneuver a hundred times. Averting her eyes, she gave him a quiet, subdued thanks. He watched her turn away and wondered if she'd been as affected by their nearness as he was. He brushed aside the crazy notion. No, she'd told him once that she didn't care for cowboys.

"Can I ride now?" Cody asked, his brown eyes sparking with eagerness.

"Sure," Marty said. Her gaze met Joe's briefly, and he read gratitude in the dark depths. "I'll help you up."

She lifted her son into Joe's waiting arms. Their hands brushed, his arm bumped her shoulder, her arm grazed his thigh. Neither spoke an apology. Neither looked the other in the eye. They both concentrated on Cody's safety, settling him firmly between Joe and the saddle horn. Joe wrapped one arm around Cody's middle and kept the other hand firmly on the reins.

"Feel okay?" he asked.

Cody nodded.

"We're fine." Joe gave Marty a nod. Slowly she stepped away, her arms crossed over her chest, a worried frown creasing her forehead. He couldn't blame her. If he had a kid, he wasn't sure he'd ever let his son out of his sight, much less hand over his child to someone else's care and protection. But he knew with a certainty born of determination that he wouldn't let harm come to Cody again.

To accustom Cody to the height and gentle shifting motions of the horse, Joe went over the fundamentals of riding in a gentle voice. "Do you know which is your left hand?"

"I'm not a baby."

Joe smiled. "Good. Bart knows his left and right hooves, too."

A tiny giggle escaped Cody.

"Put your hand on the reins, then. You can help me tell Bart where to go."

Cody settled his hand on top of Joe's. Sweat clung to the little boy's warm, clammy skin. Cody's obvious trust touched a protective chord in Joe. This little guy believed in him. As he hoped his own child would have. A nerve along his spine twisted. With that familiar pain came an urgent need to not disappoint this kid.

He cleared his throat. "When you want to go left, you simply pull the reins in that direction." Joe moved his hand accordingly, Cody following, and Bart turned his head and stepped toward the watering trough.

"Whoa!" Cody clasped Joe's hand, his fingers clinging to him.

"Whoa," Joe echoed, his voice low and steady as he pulled back on the reins. "It's okay, Cody. Bart was just following orders. He'll do whatever we tell him."

Cody remained silent for a minute. Then he pushed Joe's hand toward the right. When Bart stepped in that direction, Cody gave a nervous laugh.

"Good," Joe said. "Now what?"

"How do you make him go there?" Cody pointed straight ahead, toward the open field.

"That's even easier. Squeeze Bart with your legs. Not too much now." Joe gave the horse the signal, and they plodded forward. Bart's hooves clomped against the hard-packed earth. "Okay, you tell him where to go."

Cody shifted Joe's hand from left to right, and the horse obeyed each command. Together, the three of them zig-zagged across the field. The sun felt warm on Joe's back, the air crisp on his skin. The brittle grass cracked beneath each hoof. When they reached the far side of the pasture, Joe pulled back on the reins.

"How was that?"

"Oh, boy!" Cody bounced his hiney in the saddle. "Can we go faster?"

"Let's get used to this first. If you think you can handle it, I'll let you hold the reins by yourself."

"Yeah, yeah, I can do it." He reached for the leather reins.

"Easy," Joe cautioned. "You don't want to startle the horse."

"Sorry." Carefully this time, Cody took the reins in his hands.

Bart bobbed his head and plunged his nose toward the grass.

Cody fell forward over the saddle horn, stretching his arms out over the horse's neck, and called, "Help!

Daddy!'' His little body shifted to the side of the saddle. He dug his tiny fingers into the horse's mane. ''Joe!''

Joe already had a hand on the boy's back, his fingers curling through Cody's belt loop. But he paused, a roar sounding in his ears. What had Cody called him?

His pulse hammering, he held the boy around the middle and closed his hand over Cody's. ''It's okay. Just show him who's boss. Pull back on the reins firmly.'' The gelding lifted his head while chomping on the dry grass. ''There you go. That's it.''

Cody slumped back against Joe's belly.

''He wanted a bite to eat, is all,'' Joe explained, trying to keep a rein on his stampeding emotions. A cold chill swept through his veins. Cody had called him by his name. Not ''Daddy.'' Had the kid's memory returned? Where else would he have heard Joe? Marty had been careful not to call him that when Cody was around.

Joe wanted to ignore the incident, pretend it hadn't happened. But he couldn't.

''Cody?'' He swallowed the hard lump in his throat. ''What did you call me just then?''

The boy's body became rigid. ''Nothin'.''

Gently, Joe clasped the boy's shoulders and turned him around. He gave the boy a stern look. ''You know who I am, don't you?''

''Daddy,'' Cody said, his voice high-pitched and unsure.

A crack as wide as the Grand Canyon split Joe's heart in two. ''Tell me. Say it again.''

God, he wanted the kid to call him daddy and mean it, believe it, trust in that simple connection between them. He held his breath, waiting, hoping, praying.

Cody ducked his head and whispered, ''Joe.''

A weight of despair crashed down on him, smothering the air trapped in his lungs. A searing pain ripped through him. The charade was over.

* * *

"He knows?" Marty whispered, glancing over her shoulder to where her son had disappeared into the house for a cold drink.

Not trusting his voice, Joe nodded.

"But how?"

He shrugged.

"When did he regain his memory?" she asked as she paced back and forth beside the horse stalls. Her brown, scuffed boots kicked up bits of straw, the sound muffled by the dirt floor and the loud beating of Joe's heart.

He thought back to the moment Cody had called out his name. "I think he's known for a while and has been pretending."

Marty stopped and turned. She stared at him, her eyes glassy and hard. "But why?"

"He had his reasons, I guess. Just as we did."

"Did he tell you this?"

"Not in so many words. He acted like it was a secret. Like he was trying to cover up his blunder." A cold, empty vacuum seemed to suck the life right out of him. With resignation, he added, "He knows I'm not his dad."

Marty thrust a hand through her tangled hair. "What do we do now?" Her voice sounded strained.

"What has to be done," he stated flatly, his throat constricted by emotions he hadn't expected or wanted. The warm scents of hay, oats and leather offered a familiar comfort, but nothing could soothe this pain. At least he'd have this ranch, his empty home, and all its haunting memories.

Her brown eyes filled with tears. "Joe—"

"It's for the best." He cut her off and turned away, unable to meet her watery gaze without taking her in his arms, holding her, feeling her against him one last time. If he did, he didn't think he'd ever be able to let her go. But he had to.

For support, he leaned against Bart's stall. The gelding nuzzled his shoulder, and Joe shrugged him off. He wanted to be alone. He wanted to tend his wounds and get over this as quickly as possible. But he had a feeling it would take longer than he wanted. In fact, he wasn't sure he'd ever get over Cody. Or Marty. And the impact they'd had on him.

"You said yourself that there could never be anything between us." His voice sounded stronger than his weak heart. He knew the right look from Marty would dissolve his conviction. It would only delay their goodbyes. And make it that much more difficult.

"You were right," he continued. "We don't want to fill Cody with empty hopes. We can't go on like this. Still pretending. It's wrong."

The words sounded hollow in his own ears. He wanted Marty to say she'd been wrong, she'd made a mistake, that there could be a future between them. But he knew he was only kidding himself. He was only casting a bare hook into the Dead Sea. Marty wasn't looking for someone to come into her life. She'd been burned by a bad marriage. He knew he couldn't offer anything better. He had to face reality. Like Cody.

"I'll talk to him," she said. "Maybe we can—"

"That won't change facts." He took the hard line, because he knew it was right. But that didn't make it easier. "He's too attached. He *wants* me to be his father. We both know that won't happen." He forced his gaze to remain steady, even though his voice wavered. His resolve remained firm. Twin bright spots appeared on Marty's cheeks as she blinked away the unshed tears in her eyes. "We can't pretend anymore, Marty. It's not right. Cody has a father. I'm not him. I can't be."

Silence pounded between them, the quiet filled with unspoken words, undeclared feelings. Better left unsaid, Joe thought. Then a gentle hand touched his arm. His insides shook as he fought for control over his emotions.

"Thank you," she said, a heaviness that he'd never heard entering her voice. "You can't know how much you've meant to us. What you've done to help us. The way you... The influence you've had on Cody. Well, you've really helped him."

Words stuck in his throat. He wanted to tell her how they'd helped him face the past. But, of course, he'd never be able to pay the debt he owed his dead wife and unborn child. He'd never forgive himself. He didn't deserve it. Taking on another family would only set him up for failure. Caring for another family wouldn't dissolve his responsibility to Samantha and his unborn child.

Another swollen pause came between him and Marty.

Finally he gave a slight nod. "I better say goodbye."

Marty watched her son give Joe a tender hug. Cody wrapped his arms around Joe's neck and held on tight. Later, she'd have to talk with Cody about his little charade.

As if he'd aged another ten years, the white lines creasing the tanned skin around Joe's eyes deepened like empty creek beds during a drought. The brackets carving his cheeks pinched his mouth into a razor-thin line. He knelt in the dirt beside her son and hiked up the little chaps around Cody's slim hips, then ruffled his hair.

"You take care of your momma, you hear?" The heavy darkness had left his voice to be replaced by a forced cheerfulness.

Cody nodded, his eyes solemn and wide as if he sensed something more than a see-you-later goodbye. This one, Marty knew, would be permanent. It was for the best, as Joe had said. But why did her heart ache? Why did her pulse skitter with a moment of panic? Why did she doubt the wisdom of walking out of Joe's life?

Slowly, Joe stood. Marty held out a hand for her son. "Let's go home, Cody."

"Isn't Daddy—"

She gave him a stern look.

"Joe coming?"

"Not this time. This is *his* home."

"But—"

"We'll discuss it later, Cody." Her grip tightened on his little hand. Reluctantly her gaze met Joe's. For the last time.

A hard mass swelled in her chest, making each breath ragged. Her eyes burned. The blue of his eyes deepened to the color of midnight. "'Bye, Joe."

She waited for him to respond. She wanted to hear his voice once more and memorize the rough quality. But he remained silent. More than anything she wished he'd grab her and kiss her. One last time. But she knew he wouldn't. He'd told her he wouldn't cross that line again, not without her permission. And she couldn't—wouldn't—take the chance of reaching out to him.

Quickly she turned toward the car, needing to escape before she folded in on herself.

But Cody stopped in his tracks and pulled her to a sudden halt. He looked over his shoulder at Joe. "You're comin' to my birthday party, aren't you?" His tiny voice echoed through the barnyard.

"We'll see, sport."

"Come on, Cody." She tugged him forward as a sob broke in her chest. She knew Joe was right. Cody was too attached to this lonesome cowboy. So was she.

Chapter Eight

"How long have you known about Joe, Cody?" Marty leaned across the twin bed and rested on one elbow. She watched her son twist the cotton sheets between his tiny fingers.

He shrugged, his Winnie-the-Pooh pajamas stretching across his shoulders as if he'd suddenly outgrown them. Evening shadows from the night-light in the corner shaded his face, making him appear far older than his five-going-on-six years. Scout lay curled up next to him, his chin resting on his paws, his soulful eyes sensing no one wanted to play fetch anytime soon.

Marty put a hand on Cody's ankle, her fingers circling his baby-soft skin. A mother's job was to protect her son from pain. Unfortunately, she hadn't done a very good job. Her heart ached for him, for all he'd lost in his young life, for all he yearned for. She wished she could make his sorrow and frustration disappear. But she'd learned through experience that it wasn't that easy.

"I know you want a daddy, Cody, one that's here every

day, one that pays attention to you. Like Joe. But you already have a father.''

His long, swooping lashes hid his expression.

''Your daddy loves you very much.'' She knew deep down Flint did, but he couldn't get past his rough-and-tough ego to show it, and he couldn't set aside his own dreams to spend time with his son, who should mean more to him than a damn championship belt buckle. No matter what she thought of her ex-husband, she believed it was important for her son to know his daddy loved him.

Cody's hands balled into tight little fists.

''Look at me, sweetheart.''

A tear trickled down his pudgy, freckled cheek. He sniffed.

With a trembling finger, she wiped at the tear before lifting his watery gaze to meet hers. His tired, forlorn eyes sparked a blaze of anger in her. Not toward Cody. But toward her ex. ''Cody, sweetheart—''

''No he doesn't. Not like Joe.''

''Joe was—is…'' How could she explain how a stranger had acted more like a father than his own ever had? How could she justify Joe's actions? Or Flint's? She knew the simple answer: Joe was a caring, gentle man. One with a ghost haunting him.

But had he only acted as Cody's father out of some kind of remorse for his dead wife?

She doubted that. There had been more. Much more between all of them.

But it was over now.

''Momma,'' Cody said, drawing her thoughts back to the present. She looked into his tear-filled eyes and felt her guard drop, her resolve melt. ''I wanna 'nvite Joe to my birthday party.''

She nodded. She couldn't—wouldn't—talk him out of it. Because secretly she wanted Joe to come. She wanted to see him again. She already missed him, his gentle way of tucking her son in bed, his consistent concern for her, his warm, caring smile.

But she had to prepare them both for the very real possibility that he might not want to come. After all the disappointments they'd suffered because of Flint, they should be accustomed to it. But in such a short time, Joe had spoiled them. He'd shown them the true nature of an honest, responsible man. He'd proven through deed after deed that they could depend on him, count on him to be there when he promised. He'd never backed down on his word. Slowly, they'd placed their tentative, fragile trust in his care. And he hadn't abused it or broken their faith. Yet.

This was different, though. This required no obligation. This was a simple choice. Yes or no. She wasn't sure she wanted to take the risk of being rejected by Joe. Somehow, she knew it would hurt more than Flint's.

"Cody," she said in a soft voice, "he might not want to come."

"Sure he will. Joe loves us."

"No, Cody. He thought you believed he was your dad. So, he acted like one for you. To help you get your memory back. That was all. Love takes time to grow." They hadn't known each other long enough. Or had they? Doubting her own heart, she said, "We don't know him well enough for that to have developed."

"I love Joe," he said simply. "Don't you?"

Her throat tightened. She denied the flutter of truth in her breast. "I—I appreciate all he did for us. For you. He's a nice man."

She held back all his other attributes, folding them into her heart for safekeeping. How could she explain her high regard, her respect for Joe, without getting her son's hopes up?

"He wouldn't have done it if he hadn't loved us," Cody stated adamantly.

Out of the mouths of babes, she thought. Could some part of Joe really care about her son? About her? Once again, hope sprang within her like a sprig of bright green grass after a hard winter. Too afraid to believe, she trampled it with common sense. He'd never said he cared.

Or had he?

Had he shown them what words could never convey? Had he reached out the only way he knew how? Only for her to slap away his love, reject him, because he was a cowboy and she was afraid?

Regret twisted together with guilt like two strands of a barbed wire to tear at her conscience. They had to invite him. She'd pray he would come. She'd try not to get her hopes up. She didn't want to be disappointed again. Not by Joe.

The invitation arrived the following Thursday. It was a cold, wet day that kept Joe from working on rotten fence posts or riding his gelding away from the thoughts that plagued him. He sat at the breakfast table and listened to rain pelt the windows. Rivulets ran down the pane glass like Marty's quiet, heartfelt tears. He held the red envelope in his hands, recognized the awkward block print and felt his chest contract.

It had been almost a full week since he'd seen Cody. Or Marty. The time apart had not eased the ache inside him. If anything, he missed them more. In fact, he realized now how he'd grown dependent on the times he'd spent with them, how he'd looked forward to going to their house, even when he had to get up before the crack of dawn to do his chores around the ranch.

He'd actually started to look forward to meals again. For the past five years he'd eaten just to stay alive. As if his taste buds had died, he'd barely tasted anything. Right after his wife's death, he'd eaten most of his meals at restaurants, unable to open the refrigerator to look at the food she'd last bought, unwilling to use the dishes she'd adored, incapable of facing the deathly quiet of his house. Then he'd begun to watch other families, fathers holding small children's hands, mothers bottle-feeding tiny babies. His grief at seeing such things eventually trapped him at home, locked in his own private hell.

When he'd first met Marty and her son, he'd felt awkward sitting at their breakfast table, pretending to be a family. But as time wore on he'd come to cherish those moments, clasping hands during Cody's shy prayers, helping the little boy fill his plate, watching Marty cut her son's meat. And the banter. They'd shared unimportant, silly happenings from their days. Cody had talked about school, who'd gotten in trouble, who'd pushed whom on the playground, what letter of the alphabet they'd studied. Marty had shared her eagerness to do more at work, her dream of one day returning to school to get her teaching degree. It had been a simple time of togetherness that he'd come to love. And miss.

He missed Cody's eager-to-please smile, playing fetch with the little boy and his dog, tucking the kid in bed at night. Like a real dad. But he didn't want to pretend anymore. He wanted the real thing.

Over the past few days he'd had time to think about his own actions, if his motives had been wrong in trying to help the kid's memory return. Had he been living out his own fantasy? Pretending, like Cody, that this was his family?

The painful conclusion he'd reached told him no. He'd cared for the kid. He'd wanted to help. He'd wanted to be a part of his life.

But worse, Joe realized he'd cared for Marty more than

he'd ever thought possible. At first, her gruff independence had grated on him but soon it garnered his respect. Later, he'd glimpsed a softer side, a tenderness that had captured his heart.

He hadn't been cautious enough. Before he'd known it, she had wiggled her way past his defenses and burrowed deep into his soul. He needed her, like he needed air to breathe. In a few short weeks she'd restored a part of him he'd thought lost forever. He'd learned to smile once more.

Now, he might not find the strength to do so again.

Ripping open the end of the envelope, he skimmed the invitation to Cody's birthday party. Was this her attempt to reach out to him? Or was it her inability to convince her son that their pretend family was finished?

Whichever, he knew he couldn't go back. He couldn't get Cody's hopes up, he couldn't face Marty, knowing she didn't want another cowboy who might crush her dreams. And he couldn't torture himself.

He'd had his one chance at a family. He'd tossed it away as easily as Flint had his. Pretending was just that—pretending. In real life, he'd failed. He should never forget that. Never. Guilt clawed at him. He couldn't replace his wife and son with Marty and Cody. How could he turn his back on those memories and enjoy life again when their lives were over...forever?

Staring down at the balloons and confetti on the colorful invitation, he thought of his own son. He'd never had a birthday, much less a party. He'd never opened packages and blown out candles. Joe's empty arms ached with the inability to hold his son...as he'd held Cody.

If he'd had to R.S.V.P. in person, he knew he wouldn't have had the strength to say no to the invitation. But luckily, isolated in his own home, he could toss the card away, even if it was one of the hardest things he'd ever done.

But he could never forget.

* * *

The doorbell rang, and Cody rushed for it like a child waiting for Santa to arrive. Marty reached the entryway just as he pulled open the door, his little face expectant, a smile widening his cheeks.

"Happy Birthday!" Jason Tuttle, one of his schoolmates, called, and shoved a gift toward him.

"Oh, hi." Cody's disappointment knifed Marty.

Plastering on a smile of her own, she welcomed the child to the party, waved at the parents in the car and shut the door. Already five children had arrived. But Joe hadn't. He hadn't called, either. And she doubted he would.

"Why don't y'all go play in Cody's room with the others?" she suggested, giving her son a gentle push in that direction. "We'll have cake and ice cream when everyone gets here."

Cody glanced at her, a hopeful look piercing her soul. "Will *he* come, Momma?"

She brushed back a shock of his dark hair. She knew her son was asking about Joe. Somehow, it didn't seem odd that he didn't ask about his own father. Joe had become Cody's hero. His real father had never held that honor. "I don't know, Cody. He was probably busy, catching up on chores. You know he's been gone from his ranch quite a bit."

"Because of us." Hurt snuffed a tiny spark of optimism out of his eyes.

Marty felt her own shoulders sag under the weight of regret. She knew it would be a long, heartbreaking day. Cody followed his friend down the hallway, scuffing his boots against the carpet as he went.

The window beckoned to her, and she couldn't help pulling the sheer curtains to one side and glancing out the front. Her gaze scanned the vacant street. Sunlight shimmered off the concrete. There was no sign of his faded red pickup, and in spite of the unusually warm day she felt a cold chill ripple through her veins.

Joe wouldn't come, she reminded herself. She'd known all along. She'd told herself that each night before she went to bed, her thoughts heavy but her heart holding out till the last second. It was for the best. They needed to get on with their own lives now.

Resigned to the inevitable, she let the curtain fall back into place and headed for the kitchen. She put six blue candles around the miniature horse and cowboy that teetered precariously atop Cody's cake. Hot tears pressed against the backs of her eyes. She leaned her head back, let out a whispered breath, and forced the tears to remain at bay. She wouldn't cry over another cowboy. She wouldn't.

And she wouldn't ruin Cody's special day with what-if's and regrets.

Lowering her chin with determination, she rolled her shoulders, straightened her spine and moved the birthday cake to the kitchen table beneath the red, yellow and green balloons hanging from the light fixture. She'd twisted multicolored crepe paper to the four corners of the room. Along the wall, she'd hung a sign that read, Happy Birthday, Cody! She set out the cowboy paper plates and napkins.

Before she called the boys to come for cake and ice cream, she went to the phone and dialed another one of Flint's friends. If nothing else, maybe she could reach her ex-husband before Cody's birthday ended.

Joe saddled the blood bay. The musty odor of hay twitched his nose. He slapped a leather strap through a metal ring on the saddle and yanked it tight. His motions jerked with irritation. He knew what day it was. He knew exactly what was happening this very minute. And dammit, he couldn't stop thinking about it, imagining it, wondering what it would be like to be there. So, he'd decided to ride off from his troubling thoughts, to feel the wind against his face, the pounding force beneath him, and let the sky swallow him whole.

But instead of leading Bart toward the open pastureland of gold-tinged fields, he walked the gelding to the trailer, loaded him in and headed to town.

He didn't stop to question his sanity or ponder the consequences. He simply knew it was the right thing to do. Whatever pain he had to endure no longer mattered. But Cody did. And so did Marty.

Thirty minutes later he rang her doorbell. He heard the muted sound through the wood and leaded glass. Stepping back, he waited, his sweating palms stuffed into his back pockets. Questions and doubts spiraled together. Had he made a mistake? Would it be better for everyone concerned if he'd stayed away? How could he when Cody needed him? When Marty had invited him?

He knew receiving the invitation hadn't been a mistake. Cody hadn't surreptitiously sent it. The kid wouldn't have known Joe's address. So, Marty had sent it for a reason. Had it been to appease her son? Or had she truly wanted him to join in the festivities?

When no one answered the door, his brows slanted down the same angle of his Stetson's tilted brim. Where were they? Had he misread the invitation? Was the party someplace else? Or had he gotten the time wrong?

Had he missed the party?

Disappointment twisted his gut into a knot. He'd pulled the information from memory, because the invitation had long since been tossed with leftovers and fast-food sacks into the trash and hauled to the dump. Hoping he hadn't been wrong, he punched the peach-colored lighted button once more. If no one answered, he guessed he'd head back home.

The door swung open, and his gaze fell on a flushed Marty. Her dark eyes widened, her mouth formed a small *O*. Her hair looked disheveled, as if tossed by the wind. Her cheeks were bright pink. And her mouth looked far too kissable. "Joe," she said, her voice breathless. "You came."

Suddenly unsure of his reasons for coming, he nodded. "Am I still invited?"

"Of course!" She swung the door wider, hooked a lock of long, dark silky hair behind her ear and gave him the warmest smile he'd ever seen. "Come on in. Cody will be delighted."

From the sheen in her dark eyes, he could tell she was, too. His heart pounded until he thought his chest would burst. He stepped inside and doffed his hat, holding it in his hands. His pulse spasmed.

"Did I come at a bad time?" he asked, noticing her breasts heave beneath her white T-shirt with each breath. His gaze shifted lower to the faded blue jeans that hugged her slim figure as he wanted to.

"No, no. I've just been chasing seven boys." She grinned, and a dimple winked in her cheek.

"Not a co-ed party?"

She laughed. "Didn't you know? Girls are gross. You know, cooties."

"Not in my book." Their gazes locked and a ripple of excitement passed between them.

"Mom's are different, though," she said, averting her eyes.

"Uh-huh," he muttered, his throat tight, his gaze skimming down her soft curves with renewed hunger.

The silence stretched between them and he noticed the quiet stillness inside the house had a beat of its own that was steadier and slower than his own heart's. "Where's Cody? Is the party over?"

She blew a breath toward her bangs. "I wish. Scout's keeping them busy in the backyard. I should—"

"Sure," he said, inclining his head for her to go ahead.

She paused at the back door, her hand on the knob, and looked over her shoulder at him. Her chocolate-colored eyes softened. "Thanks for coming, Joe."

He didn't know what to say. He didn't think he could manage a word if he tried. Glancing down at his empty hands, he said, "I didn't bring a present. This was sort of a last-minute decision."

She nodded as if she understood.

"You'll be gift enough." Her voice dropped with, "His father didn't call."

"I'm sorry." The words came automatically, but they held more meaning than he could ever express. His muscles tensed as he wished he could club Flint for being an idiot.

"Me, too. But I'm glad you're here, though." Marty touched his shirt sleeve in a brief gesture of thanks, then withdrew her hand. The nerves along his skin cried out for her, but he silenced them with the knowledge that she didn't mean it personally. She was glad for her son.

"I did bring a surprise," he offered, remembering the trailer parked out front.

Her narrow brow arched. "What's that?"

"Bart. I thought the kid might like a ride on his birthday."

"Oh, he'll love that!"

By eight o'clock that evening, Marty felt as if she'd been dragged around Fort Worth by her heels. Her back ached, her head hurt. But she'd never been happier in her life.

With Joe's help, she'd put an exhausted but deliriously joyful little boy to bed. That afternoon, Joe had given Cody and his friends short rides around the backyard on his horse. It had been the most successful party any six-year-old ever dreamed of.

Thanks to Joe.

That simple, honest phrase seemed to roll through her mind more and more often these days. She never thought she'd be grateful to a man, much less dependent on one. She no longer resented his help...or him. Every time she saw him, her respect grew. She knew she was treading in dangerous waters.

She stuffed a wad of paper napkins into the trash bag he held. Over the sickly sweet smell of icing, she caught a whiff of his scent, deeply masculine, distinctively cowboy and uniquely Joe. She wanted to lean closer, but she didn't dare.

She stared into those deep blue eyes and knew the heart of the man who'd helped her son, who'd helped her finally admit she wanted, maybe even needed, a man in her life. This man.

Her heart pounded like a deaf rock 'n' roll drummer. She licked her dry lips and retreated to the sink, knowing she was playing with fire. Could she take a chance on Joe? Would he even welcome her interest in pursuing something between them? Or had his past heartbreak closed him forever to the possibility of love?

The kitchen smelled of melted vanilla ice cream, charcoal from the barbecue and greasy hot dogs. Scout's nails clicked against the linoleum as he licked cake crumbs off the floor. A comfortable silence fell over the room, wrapping Marty in a blanket of security, something she rarely, if ever, felt as a single mother.

She busied herself washing dishes. The warm, sudsy water soothed her frazzled nerves. She heard Joe cinch the garbage bag, take it to the garage and lock the door. Family sounds, gentle, familiar and sweet, enveloped her heart and made her yearn for things she'd once thought impossible.

A heavy sigh and groan drew her attention. Over her shoulder, she saw Joe collapse into a slat-backed chair. Beneath the buttery yellow starched shirt, his broad, strong shoulders slumped forward with fatigue. He ran his fingers through his rumpled hair and stretched out his long legs, crossing his ankles. The toes of his boots pointed toward the bright, iridescent lights. His features lifted in a sexy smile that had her insides and doubts thawing like ice cream left on the counter.

"Tired?" she asked, a grin stealing its way across her lips.

"Uh-huh." He crossed his arms over his chest. He looked natural sitting there in her kitchen. Part of her wished he could stay. "It's been a long day."

"You should have been here from the start." Her smile wilted as she realized her slip of the tongue. In one careless moment she'd whisked away the comfortable ease between them. "I m-mean—"

"I know," he said, his voice even, his gaze as intense as a red-hot poker. "It's okay. I wish I had been." Seconds ticked by before he said in a low voice, "I wasn't going to come. But I couldn't get it out of my head. Then I just got in the truck and headed this way."

His struggle, she realized, had matched her own over sending the invitation. Somehow that thought pacified her worries. She'd felt a kinship with this man ever since that very first day when she'd left the emergency room, anxious and tired, only to find him waiting for her, for Cody. Yet the bond between them had grown over these past weeks, his gentle compassion toward Cody and herself had touched her. Never had her ex ever shown such care and concern. Joe's presence had lifted part of the burden of parenthood temporarily from her shoulders. He'd opened her mind...and heart...to new possibilities.

She wanted to know Joe better, understand what made him tick, delve into the mystery behind his guarded smile and reluctant involvement. He reminded her of an ice-covered lake, cold, hard and forbidding on the outside, but once thawed, gentle and beautiful.

"Were you worried about why I'd invited you?" she asked, hoping to know if he thought about her as often as she did him.

"Partly." His lips pressed together. The light from his blue eyes dimmed. "I didn't know if I could handle it."

The deepness of his voice drew her across the room to his side as she wiped her hands then discarded the towel. A chill seeped into her bones. Pulling his boots back toward him, he shifted, the muscles in his arms tightening. The lines in his face hardened, as if they'd been carved in granite. She sank into the chair beside him.

"What do you mean?" she asked, her casual tone hiding the sudden coiling tension inside her.

For a brittle moment he said nothing. The air seemed to crackle with static electricity. His features were icy, his shoulders turned slightly away from her. His cold gaze seemed focused on something distant and elusive.

"My wife," he said, his voice staccato, "wasn't the only one killed in that car crash. "My son—" his voice broke "—was, too."

The words roared through her mind like a train bound for nowhere, the screaming wheels carrying her with it. Her breath caught in her throat. Suddenly she felt as if she were being hurled along the tracks at an incredibly dangerous speed. She couldn't stop what she'd started. She couldn't put the brakes to what he was about to say.

He tilted his head, and a shadow fell like a shroud across

his features. Then he stood, scraping back the chair, and walked across the room, his boot heels clumping hollowly across the linoleum.

"Oh, Joe." She stared after him, unable to find the energy to rise. "No."

His mouth pulled to the side. The muscles in his throat contracted. His features contorted. "He died with her."

Marty felt the weight of his words sink her deeper into her seat, darkening her vision, and pulling at her heartstrings. Scalding tears burned her eyes and throat. Now, she understood. After all these weeks, she now knew why Joe had helped her son. She'd thought only the memory of his wife had stood between them. But there was more. So much more. She felt a chasm open, the gulf separating them, tearing them apart. Her son was their only fragile link.

"How old was he?" she asked, her voice weak, even though she had an awful feeling she knew the answer.

"He hadn't been born."

Startled, her chest tightened. She'd expected him to say his son had been Cody's age. Then it hit her. His son *would have been* five-going-on-six.

"It was my fault, you see. Mine. I should have been there. I should have been driving her that night. She'd met me in Dallas for a damn rodeo. It had seemed important then. One of many important rodeos leading me to my third championship." He spoke in a clipped tone. "It was late when she headed home. Raining. She'd asked me to skip the next rodeo in Amarillo. To come home. To spend some time with her. To help her get things ready for the baby." He paused, licked his dry lips and stuck his hand out in front of him as if testing the air. "I remember putting my hand on her stomach, feeling the baby kick, her belly move." His fingers curled into a tight fist. "But I said no. I had to go. It was important. I needed the points. I needed this ride.''

He blinked, and his voice changed, deepened, became more matter-of-fact. "Samantha was far enough along in her pregnancy for them to determine it was a boy.'' His voice came to her muffled, tired, devoid of emotion.

She sensed the turmoil raging inside him, saw it in his quick, shallow breaths, the tensing of muscles along his neck. His hands balled into tight fists at his sides, as if he were trying to strangle the emotions, hold back the pain— resist, restrain—as he relived the trauma in his mind's eye.

He made a noise, one she couldn't discern as a groan, a plea, or even a word, but it was a sharp sound, bitter, tragic. "I toyed with a few names for a while. Until I settled on Sam, after my wife. It seemed right.

"Samantha and I hadn't talked about names yet. I hadn't been home often enough. Maybe she'd come up with a few. I don't know. We were supposed to start shopping for the baby's room. Soon as I found some free time.''

He shoved his hands into his front pockets and hunched his shoulders as if taking a blow to his solar plexus. "I never did. I wondered what his life—Sam's—would have been like. What he would have done. How he would have talked. What it would have been like to sit him on my knee, shake his hand, hold him close.''

Like he had with Cody, Marty thought, her heart breaking.

His voice sounded husky, coarse. "I imagined him learning to walk, asking me for the car keys, going out on his first date. There's not an aspect of his life that I haven't tried to imagine. For him.''

Or for you? She wondered if it had been another form of punishment that he'd used to torture himself. But she couldn't ask him that. She remembered the heart-stopping moment when she'd seen Cody lying still in the dirt. The fear had been strong, fierce, powerful. She could only imagine how it would destroy her heart beyond repair to lose her child.

She knew then why Joe had come back today. Not for her. Not for any possibilities that only she seemed capable of seeing. Not for Cody, either. But for his own son. To face the ghost haunting him.

Marty let her tears fall then. Silent, streaming tears that seemed to pour out of her eyes like blood from an open wound. She wept for Joe. Tears of pain slipped down her cheeks, hot, bitter, countless. Her chest ached for the son who would never know the depth of his father's love, for Joe's wife and for their family ripped apart. She cried for her own son who would never have a father as wonderful and caring as Joe.

A racking sob caught in her throat. Last, she cried for herself. Because she knew she'd fallen in love with Joe. And he would never risk loving her in return.

Chapter Nine

Marty's gentle sobbing brought him back to reality. How long had it been since he'd shed a tear? How long since he'd felt anything besides deep, penetrating guilt? He'd drowned beneath other peoples' tears, flooded by their sorrow and his own remorse. To survive, he'd blocked out their weeping. But Marty's tears made him look outside his own darkness.

Shame sucked at his conscience. He hadn't meant to make her cry. He hadn't meant to sour this sweet celebration day. Once again, his selfishness had caused someone else pain.

Her soft tears touched him in a way he hadn't experienced in years. If ever.

Maybe it was because for the first time in five long, lonely years he'd let someone get close to him. Maybe because he knew Marty cried for him. He felt it in his bones, heard it in each of her ragged breaths, sensed it in the depths of his soul. When had anyone cried for *him?*

He didn't deserve it. With a quick snap of his shoulders,

he turned. Her tears felt like blood on his hands. He wanted to shake her, stop those damn tears, block out the sound of her gentle weeping.

But the sight of her bent over, her hands cupping her face, her hair falling forward like a thick veil, made his steps falter. She looked alone, bereft. A helpless isolation closed in on him. This time, he knew he couldn't ignore her pain. This time, he couldn't turn away. He had to reach out.

But it took every ounce of strength he owned.

Uncertain what to do or say, he moved toward her. He felt as if he walked through thick, boggy mud. Blood pounded in his ears with each hastened beat of his heart. His hands trembled. His insides wrenched. For one moment he wanted to feel that deeply, that completely, that openly again. Five years ago, out of necessity, he'd shut down his emotions, only allowing guilt to seep out and saturate the rest of his life. Jealousy stabbed at him now. For in Marty, he saw what he wanted—needed—to feel. It tore at his heart, with claws so sharp, they ripped through the layers he'd built over the years.

Reverently, he knelt in front of her. With the crook of his finger, he tipped her chin toward him. Her face was bleak with sorrow. Slowly, carefully, he wiped at her tears, smoothing his thumb along her cheek, over the tender skin beneath her eyes. Her nose had turned bright red. Her eyes appeared glassy, teardrops spiking her dark lashes.

"Don't cry," he whispered.

Her gaze sought his, looking far into the recesses of his soul. With an urgency, she closed a hand over his wrist when he would have backed away. Her lips glistened like early morning dew. "I can't help it. I didn't know you'd been through...suffered...so much." Her voice cracked. "I'm sorry." She tilted her head and leaned into his palm, her flesh warm and wet against him. Softly, like the brush of a butterfly's wing, she kissed the inside of his hand. His insides fluttered. "I'm sorry," she said again and again. "I should have guessed. I should have known."

"How?" His thumb rubbed along her trembling bottom lip. "It's not something I talk about. You're the first—" His tight throat cut off the rest of his explanation.

"But I... You were forced into an...awkward...horrible situation. It was cruel. I'm sorry, Joe. I shouldn't have asked you to help with Cody."

He leaned closer, pressing his forehead to hers, forcing her watery gaze to meet his. "I volunteered, remember?"

"But—"

He shook his head, rocking his brow against hers in a gentle, lulling motion. He tasted her mint-flavored breath, inhaled her breezy scent that turned his senses inside out. "I wanted to help." His voice became stronger. "In the end, you helped me."

"I did?" she asked, her eyes blinking.

"I'd been wallowing in my guilt. Guess I still am. But I needed to see that life, today and tomorrow, is more important than yesterday. I can't change what happened. God, I wish I could. I'd give my life for theirs. But I can't. Still, I can damn well help someone else. My life isn't over yet."

"Maybe it's just beginning," she said. Her words lingered between them like a warm breath.

Then she shifted, angling her mouth over his, then pressed her lips against his. She was hot, and he melted into her, giving in to the moment, the need, the want. He forgot all his doubts and resistance and let her catch him up in the heat.

He lost himself in the feel of her. Her lips tugged at him eagerly, hungrily. He wanted this time to last forever, stretching into eternity with Marty in his arms, warm, vibrant and willing. The uncertainty and fragility of life made him hold her tighter.

His fingers curled toward her jawline, pulling her closer and closer, until his tongue glided across hers, tasting her, luxuriating in the textures and sensations that made her unique. He swallowed her sigh, savored her sweetness, embraced the very essence of her. It was as if they shared their souls.

He knew in that instant what he could no longer deny. He loved her. Loved her strength, her vulnerability, her compassion. In the wash of that hopeful revelation, a bittersweet reality rolled over him. He knew his own limitations. With love came responsibility. *Maybe* he could be dependable. *Maybe*. But did he dare take the chance? Not that he cared about himself, but he never wanted to disappoint Marty or her son. He never wanted to fail them. As her ex had. As Joe had his own family.

The telephone jangled. He pulled away from her, kissed the tip of her nose, then smiled. She returned his smile and his spirit soared. Touching her swollen lips, she muttered, "Somebody's got really bad timing."

He nodded. But he wondered if it wasn't fate stepping in, knowing his limitations better than he did, punishing him for his past sins.

By the fourth ring, she lifted the receiver, sniffed and said hello. Immediately a frown emerged along her brow. Her back straightened. "It's Cody's birthday."

There was no accusation, no condemnation, but a sad resignation that told Joe her ex-husband had finally received one of her many messages. She looked to him, and he read a swell of emotional turmoil in the depths of her brown eyes.

"He's asleep," she said, her voice tight, after another pause.

For a few anxious minutes Joe turned away, pretending

not to listen, studying the blackness of the night outside the window. He wanted to give them privacy, as much as a divorced couple needed, but his ears strained for any nuance of weakness or longing in her voice. With Flint, she seemed to have an impenetrable wall, a fortress, that Joe knew the other cowboy could never scale. He felt grateful she'd opened the door of her heart to him. If only for a mere glimpse inside.

She paused in her phone conversation, put a hand over the receiver and said, "Joe, would you wake Cody so his dad can wish him a happy birthday?"

He nodded, and his gut tightened with jealousy. It hurt him beyond what he'd ever imagined to wake a sleepy Cody and say, "Hey, cowboy, your dad's on the phone." *Your real dad.*

Cody blinked, and the fog in his dark eyes cleared. A wisp of a smile touched his lips when he focused on Joe. Carrying the little boy into the kitchen, Joe relished the tiny hand resting on his shoulder. Marty gave her son a too bright smile, but Cody didn't return it. He held the phone to his ear and in a tinny voice said, "Hi."

There was a long pause before the boy spoke again, "Okay. Uh-huh. 'Bye." He handed the phone back to his mom and snuggled against Joe's shoulder.

Joe thought his heart would burst with love as he carried the tired birthday boy back to bed.

By the time he returned to the kitchen, Marty was saying, "Fine. I'll see you then." She hung up the phone with a decisive click.

Another flicker of jealousy flared inside him. He faced her, his brow lifted in question. With her head bent, she still had a hand on the wall phone, her back to him.

"Flint," she said, with obvious irritation. "He has no concept of when a kid goes to bed. He thinks the world revolves around him."

Joe understood her anger, yet he knew how easy it was to fall into the egocentric trap ensnaring Flint. He'd been hooked once himself. The rodeo was a wild, roller coaster ride, with ups and downs, only grinding to a halt when you were hurt. That's why so many injured cowboys kept on riding. Nobody wanted the ride to stop. It had taken a heart-wrenching tragedy to pull him out of his own self-absorption.

Or had it?

Had he only transferred his self-centeredness to something else—guilt or withdrawal from the human race? Is that what he'd been doing for the past five years under the guise of grief and guilt?

Marty had rescued him from that. In her need, he'd found a reason to live. If only for a short while.

She let out a protracted sigh. "Sorry. I didn't mean to dump on you."

He moved toward her then, laid his hands on her narrow shoulders and kneaded the tense muscles. A soft moan escaped her as she leaned back against him.

"I just get so mad at him. He never thinks about Cody. I had to track him down like a thief to tell him Cody was hurt. And you know what his response was? 'How long did he hang on before he fell?' Flint wasn't concerned about Cody at all. Now I have to locate him so Cody will think his father remembered his birthday." She rotated her neck, stretching it to the left then right. "Ah, right there," she whispered as he pressed a tender spot. "I should know by now he won't change."

"Was he at a rodeo tonight?"

Marty shrugged. "Yeah. He was in a hurry. Headed out for a celebration party. Probably with a barrel racer. He likes barrel racers. Always has."

Joe's grip on her neck and shoulders tightened. Did her ex-husband's philandering bother her? "Are you jealous?"

She laughed, the sound more caustic than humorous. "Not anymore. I'm over Flint. Have been for a long time. Our marriage died years before the divorce papers were signed. When we were married, I tried to compete..." She shook her head. "I couldn't."

Slowly he turned her to face him, his hands bracketing her shoulders. His gaze penetrated her defenses and saw the insecurities eating away at her. "Flint's a damn fool."

"Yeah. Maybe."

"Not maybe. Absolutely."

She stepped away from him before he could elaborate or show her with a sizzling kiss how attractive and desirable she was. "Well, he's coming back."

Joe's gaze narrowed with concern.

"Next weekend," she added. When she turned, he understood the turmoil in her eyes as pain. "There's a rodeo nearby. He wants to take Cody, for a birthday celebration."

Confused by her despondency, he said, "I thought you wanted him to spend time with Cody."

"I do, but..." She fell silent, biting her bottom lip. "I should be glad. But I'm not." She gave a halfhearted smile that never erased the anguish in her eyes. "He'll probably cancel. Cody will get his hopes up, then he'll end up disappointed. That's what happened the night we met you. Flint was supposed to be at the rodeo."

Joe's jaw clenched. He remembered the sad, lost look in Cody's expressive eyes, how he'd clung to Joe, how he'd needed a father. The bastard! How could Flint ignore his own son! Didn't he realize what a blessing he had! How could he—

Joe stopped his mental whipping of Flint. He'd been the same way once. But he'd learned a hard lesson. Only afterward, had he known what he'd lost. How could he condemn Flint, when he deserved damnation himself?

"If he does show," Marty said, her brow crinkling, her fingers twisting together, "I don't know what I'll do."

"What do you mean?" he asked, confused.

She looked up at the ceiling and released a sigh. "I can't remember the last time I was alone. Without Cody. Doesn't that sound weird? Isn't a mom supposed to enjoy her free time?"

Something in her voice tugged at him. "You won't be alone," he said automatically, stepping forward. He brushed a hair away from her eye and hooked it behind her delicate ear. "You'll be with me."

"Oh, Joe, I couldn't—"

"Impose?" he asked. "You wouldn't be. Cody will go out with his dad. And you'll go out with me."

She stared up at him, her jaw slack, her eyes like deep, dark pools, mysterious and filled with emotions he couldn't decipher. "Like a date?"

"Would that be so terrible? Isn't it about time?"

"Yes. No. I mean— I'm all confused."

He stroked the gentle curve of her jaw. "Want me to clear things up?" His gaze focused on her mouth.

She swallowed hard then licked her lips. He almost groaned aloud with wanting. "Joe, are you sure?"

"I hope Flint shows." His voice dropped to a husky level that seemed to vibrate within his chest. "I'd like to spend some time with you." He brushed one last kiss across her mouth before heading home. "Alone."

The moon was full and as luminous as a pearl positioned on black velvet. A light chill had swept into Fort Worth earlier in the day, a reminder of winter, but Marty had seen it as a promise of spring as, along the horizon, clouds had floated like gossamer curtains billowing in a cool draft. Wood smoke from the row of chimneys on Marty's street now toasted the crisp evening air.

"Will you be warm enough?" Joe asked, holding open her coat as she slipped first one arm then the other into the woolen sleeves.

"I'll be fine." She turned and smiled up at him.

He lifted her hair from inside her coat and settled her collar around her neck. Their hands brushed as she reached for the zipper. A spark of expectancy flared between them. She didn't know what this evening held in store for them. She wasn't sure what Joe wanted. But she'd decided not to question herself, him, or the moment. This once, she wanted to embrace it. She wanted to feel like a desirable woman.

"Did Cody get off okay?" he asked as he locked the door and shut it, testing the brass knob one last time for her.

She nodded, and he fell into step beside her. An icy breeze brushed across her face, and she snuggled farther into her warm coat. "Flint showed up. Half an hour late. But at least he showed. Cody didn't want to go."

"Why not?" Joe asked.

"Because he's seen the way a real father should love his son. He knows the difference in the way Flint treats him. You're his hero."

Joe's head bent forward, hiding his expression beneath the shadows cast by the brim of his Stetson.

She swallowed the bitter taste of guilt. "I reminded him Flint was his real father. Flint, of course, got mad. Which didn't help anything."

Joe squeezed her hand as if instinctively understanding her dilemma, her fears, her pain.

"I just hope everything goes okay for Cody. And that Flint remembers to help Cody with his hat and gloves. It's cold out."

"Come on, Momma." Offering a warm grin, Joe wrapped an arm around her shoulders and pulled her against the protective shelter of his body. "He'll be fine. You'll see."

She felt a blossoming inside her, unfolding her vulnerability, opening her secrets to him. It was so easy, so right, to talk to Joe, to share her fears, to relax, to simply be with him. She'd never felt this way with her ex. Joe made her crazy, chaotic days slow to a quiet, tranquil tempo. But each time he looked at her, touched her, took her hand, a current of electricity pulsed inside her.

He opened the passenger door of his truck, and she slid inside. "Before he left," she said, "Cody asked if you'd be at the rodeo, too." She gave him a warm smile and placed a hand over his heart. She felt the steady thumping beneath her palm. It made her feel secure. "You mean a lot to him." *And to me.*

"I know," he answered quietly. The moon glinted in the dark midnight depths of his eyes, making them compelling, magnetic.

After he circled the truck, he cranked the engine, giving the gas pedal a gentle prodding and the steering wheel an encouraging pat. "Did you tell him we were going out?"

She shook her head, feeling the bite of guilt again. "I couldn't. But I gave them the phone number of the restaurant. In case…"

Joe remained silent as he steered the truck down the street. "That's a good idea. You did the right thing."

"I didn't think Cody would understand about you and me going out. I wanted him to enjoy his evening with Flint. I don't want to confuse him."

"Marty," he said, "you don't owe me an explanation. You're Cody's mother. You know what's best for him. I understand." He glanced at her then, and she knew he meant what he said. "You did what was best for your son."

He fiddled with the radio, punching buttons until he

found an upbeat song. Dolly Parton's voice lilted over the airwaves.

The blast from the heater warmed Marty's toes. She'd chosen casual attire for the evening, but had spiced up her black jeans and boots with a silk shirt that made her feel sexier than usual. She hoped Joe had noticed.

She pushed her worries about hurting Joe's feelings out of her mind. He was practical, sensible. Her reasons for not telling Cody about their date had been simple—she didn't know what it meant. She didn't know what Joe was willing to offer, or what he had in mind. Right now, she didn't want to think of the future—with or without Joe. She simply wanted to be with him.

"What time will Flint have him home?" Joe asked as Dolly's last note lingered in the cab.

"Probably not till eleven or so."

He nodded. "I'll have you home before then."

Warmed by Joe's thoughtfulness, she smiled in the darkness and reached across the seat, over the brim of his Stetson lying between them, and touched his hand. She'd accused him once of being just a cowboy like her ex. But he wasn't. He was much more. He was responsible, honest and true to his word. She knew without a doubt that she'd found a good man, and relaxed when he threaded his fingers through hers to clasp her hand.

It began to mist just before ten. Occasional raindrops tapped against the hood of the car, and moisture spread like tiny threads across the windshield. A George Strait song played on the radio, the steady beat in sync with the intermittent flap of the wipers. Marty had shrugged out of her coat, and her purple silk shirt caught the light each time a car passed.

He'd noticed. Compliments had lodged in his throat all evening, but he'd worried he'd frighten her if he came on too strong. He wasn't sure where he'd thought this evening would go. But he didn't want to stop to think about it. He'd only wanted to spend each moment with Marty; completely focused on her, not consequences or repercussions.

"I didn't know we'd have to wait so long to be seated," Joe said, both hands on the wheel but itching to feel that silk shirt beneath his palm. "We better head back to your place." Disappointment welled up inside him, and he let it out on a heavy sigh. "I want you to be there when Cody gets home."

She nodded. "Did you have something else planned?"

He shrugged. "An idea."

"For us?" Eagerness lifted her voice. "What?"

Feeling the tips of his ears burn, he was grateful for the darkness. "I was going to take you dancing over at Billy Bob's. It's been a while since I've two-stepped. If you'd been brave enough, I'd have given it a go."

She glanced at her watch. "We have time. For one dance."

"Not to drive all the way over there and back. I don't want to take the chance."

"Then stop here," she said, her voice no more than a murmur. The music seemed to swallow it up.

"What?" He shot a glance at her.

"Stop here."

He looked out the window at the deserted street, the green light, the empty office buildings. "Where? At the bus stop?"

She laughed. "Sure."

"It's raining."

"Are you scared you'll melt?"

A grin tugged at his mouth.

"Haven't you ever danced in the rain?" she asked.

"No."

"Well, you should."

"Have you?" he asked, curious and envious of any man she'd danced with. Had it been Flint? His hands tightened around the steering wheel.

"No," she confessed. She sank back against the seat and closed her eyes. "Just this once let's pretend we don't have a care in the world. No responsibilities. No worries. No past or future. Just here and now. Oh, Joe, let's dance in the rain."

Hearing the longing in her voice, he cut his eyes toward her. She gave him a secretive smile that he couldn't resist. His pulse quickened, his breath catching in his chest.

Flipping on the right turn signal, he veered off the road and parked. The silence in the cab magnified until it throbbed with the beat of his heart. A slight tremor shook his hand. He found a well-worn Vince Gill tape along his dash and stuck it in the stereo. It took a moment to find the right song. When the slow, melodic chords began, he stepped out of the truck and went around to Marty's side. He opened her door and held out his hand for her. She clasped it. In that one simple gesture he felt her strength, softness and trust.

Reaching into the cab, he turned up the volume. He led her into the beam of the headlights that cut a swath out of the darkness. The concrete felt slippery beneath his boots, and sweat trickled down his spine. He circled around, watching their shadows merge, separate and fall together again. Then he waited, feeling the cool rain on his skin, dampening his shirt.

He studied the woman in front of him. Her eyes looked dark and mysterious. The mist made her hair glisten as if with fairy dust. Damp tendrils clung to her cheek. Dark, wet splotches began to form on her shirt along her shoulders and breasts. His focus narrowed on the peaks pushing against the silk. His gut burned with a need so intense he thought he'd die watching her.

Lifting one hand, he silently asked her to dance with him in the rain. She stepped into his arms, and it felt as if he'd come home.

"Joe." She smiled. His name was like music on her lips.

He pulled her close, tucking her body tightly to his, sheltering her from as much of the rain as he could. She nestled her cheek against his chest, and her hand slipped around his waist, her fingers clasping his belt loop. Her breasts, warm and inviting, teased him with her soft curves. He skimmed a hand down her side and rested his palm along her hip, aligning her against him. The fit was snug and seductive.

He wanted to lift her face to his, let the rain wash over them both, then make love first to her mouth then to the rest of her body. Not yet, he reminded himself. Maybe not ever. With what was left of his common sense, he reined in his passion, swallowed hard, and tried to remember how to two-step.

There was no one here to judge his ability, no honky-tonk regulars to be compared to, no certain steps to follow. There was only Marty and him. Only they mattered. He knew she wouldn't laugh at his attempt. She wouldn't criticize. She would catch him if he slipped. She'd match his steps. And they'd dance.

His first steps were hesitant, unsure, then he found the rhythm, and their bodies moved as one, thighs brushing, breaths merging in tiny, frosty puffs. Her musky scent, like mist off her skin, rose to envelope him. The music floated around them. He turned her this way and that, testing the boundaries of the headlights and their dancing proficiencies.

On a quick beat, he whirled her around, pressing against the dip in her back to keep her safe against him. He twirled her around in a succession of turns, and she let her head fall back. Raindrops wet her face as tiny rivulets ran into her hair. His gaze dropped to her softly curved lips. A throaty laugh rippled out of her. He loved the sound that seemed to float on the air and linger in his heart.

Tempting him with a warm, summery smile, she started singing, her voice low with a velvety texture. She overshot a few notes along the way, and he laughed along with her. Reluctantly at first, he joined in as the words came back to him about loneliness and heartbreak, fulfillment and love. Together their voices, slightly off key, harmonized as their bodies moved in one accord as if they'd danced together from the beginning of time.

As the song ended, her arms came around his neck and he lifted her off her feet. She pressed her face into his neck and whispered, "Thank you."

"Anytime," he smiled, knowing he meant it with all his heart.

Thirty minutes later Joe maneuvered the truck down her winding, rain-slick street. The stillness seemed surreal. Which struck her as odd. It was a quiet neighborhood with several young families and elderly couples. But tonight it seemed too quiet. Maybe it was the giddy feeling making her want to run amok down the middle of the street, an idiotic smile on her face. For the first time in years her body sang with energy and excitement. All because of Joe.

Then her focus narrowed to the end of the street. She saw Flint's bold, black truck parked along her curb. Her smile faded.

"He's here," she said, her hand gripping the door handle. Her mind spun with the questions Cody would ask. What would she say? How would she answer her young son?

"I see," Joe said. His profile looked troubled with his

brow bunched together, the lines angling toward his nose, and the corners of his mouth stretched taut.

As they pulled up behind Flint's gleaming chrome bumper, Marty wished her ex would pay half as much attention to his son as he did his brand new Chevy. If he'd polished and changed the oil in their marriage with such loving, tender devotion, they might have still been married. But then she wouldn't have felt like this. She glanced at Joe and a warm sensation wafted through her, making her bones liquefy. Her ex could never be as special or as wonderful to her as Joe.

His truck's headlights flashed across the back window of Flint's cab. It looked empty. Concerned, she glanced at the porch. Her ex paced along the narrow space, his hands jammed into his hip pockets, his Stetson angled low over his brow in an angry display.

"Cody must have pooped out," she said with relief. "He must be sleeping in the cab."

"Good," Joe said realistically. "There will be less complications if he doesn't see me. I'll see you to the door, then I'll let Flint carry his own kid to bed."

Something deep inside her twisted. Was it the hoarseness in his voice? Or was it her own longing to share the familiar ritual of tucking Cody into bed with Joe? It wouldn't be the same with Flint. It wouldn't have the same sweet, lullaby quality. But this once, it would be for the best.

Grateful again for Joe's understanding and wisdom, but saddened by the circumstances, she put a hand on his arm. "You're a good man, Joe Rawlins. I hope you know that."

She leaned over and pressed a kiss to his cheek. "Thank you for the evening. It was the best...ever."

He looked at her with deep, solemn eyes, then slowly one corner of his mouth lifted into a sexy grin. "My pleasure. Maybe we can do it again. Soon."

Feeling a headiness steal over her, she nodded, unable to squeeze a word out of her tight throat. Did she dare hope for something more between them?

"Where've you been?" Flint demanded as they approached, his arms crossed at his chest as he stood, like the lord of the manor, on the top step. His gaze flickered over Marty first, then narrowed and took in Joe. "Rawlins?" His tone shifted from irritated to awestruck. "Joe Rawlins?"

"Hello, Flint. It's been a while."

"Yeah." The two men shook hands.

"Hey, Marty, did you know this guy won—"

"She knows," Joe said.

"Oh, well, sure she does. Who doesn't?" Flint had that familiar I'm-gonna-be-a-champion hungry gleam in his eye. "Did y'all have trouble with your truck?"

"No," Marty answered. "Why?" Then she remembered her wet hair. Her clothes beneath her coat felt sticky and damp against her skin. She could have groaned at her blunder.

"You're all wet. Or hadn't you noticed?"

She felt a blush color her from her toes clear up to her hairline. Her skin felt prickly from the inner heat.

Joe chuckled. "My fault. We got caught without an umbrella. Should have listened to the weather forecast."

She gave him a relieved smile. "Why don't we go on inside? It's nippy out here." She rubbed her arms and huddled deeper into her wool coat. "Flint, you can carry Cody to his room."

"He's not here."

Like a bomb, silence exploded around them, echoing in Marty's ears. Fear, as black as the night, swept over her. A cold knot formed in the pit of her stomach.

"Where is he?" Joe asked, iciness chilling his words.

Flint spread his arms wide. "Hell if I know. He disappeared on me."

The words rang in her head like the recoil of a gun firing. Her knees weakened. Her heart stopped. A coppery taste filled her mouth, and she forced back the bile rising in her throat. She felt strong hands, Joe's sturdy hands, wrap around her arm and waist. She absorbed his strength, leaned into it, needed it more than she'd ever needed anything in her life. But she had to resist. This was *her* son. She had to do something. She had to think. But her thoughts slugged through a dense fog.

"What the hell do you mean, disappeared?" Joe asked for her.

Flint rubbed his hands up and down his thighs. "One minute he was in the truck babbling about some cowboy named Joe."

Marty felt her world tilt out of orbit.

Flint scuffed his boots against the wooden planks. "Now, I know Cody meant you." His voice grew louder, defensive, his gestures broader. "That's all he could talk about. I was gettin' damn tired of hearing 'Joe did this,'" he mimicked in a high-pitched voice, "and 'Joe did that.'"

"What happened to Cody?" Joe said through clenched teeth.

"I went in to pay for gas. You know, into the station and when I come out…he was gone."

"Gone?" Marty asked in a weak, agony-filled voice.

"Yeah. I mean—"

"Why didn't you call me? I gave you the number!"

Flint ducked his head. "Cody had it. I told him to put it in his pocket for safe-keeping."

A frustrated breath whooshed out of Marty.

"Did you call the cops?" Joe asked.

"No, I thought—"

"Don't." Joe grabbed Marty's purse, rummaged inside

and found her keys. He let them all inside, flipped on the lights and headed toward the kitchen with determined steps that resounded in Marty's head.

She stood in the entryway, staring at Cody's miniature football. Scout greeted her with a wagging tail and lolling pink tongue. Automatically, she reached down and grazed her fingers along his silky head. A trembling started deep inside her and spread out to her limbs until she shook all over.

"What time did all this happen?" Joe said as he returned to the den.

Flint plopped down into the leather recliner as though it was still his. "About eight o'clock." Defensively, he added, "I tried to—"

Joe cursed, the foul word carrying the impact of a punch. He grabbed Flint by the front of his shirt and jerked him to his feet. The sound of threads ripping carried across the room and spurred Marty into action.

She had to do something. She had to find her son. Cody depended on her. And her alone.

Ignoring the two men, she raced for the phone, her legs feeling wobbly and uncertain, her muscles straining with sudden fatigue. She jabbed three numbers on the phone and glared at Flint. "You let that much time go by without calling for help?"

"I didn't remember what restaurant you said," Flint said. "Didn't know you were on a hot date with Rawlins here." His voice bit into her conscience with sharp-edged accusation.

She shouldn't have forced Cody to go with Flint. She should have been here. She should have been here for her son. It was all her fault. Her world collapsed around her, sucking her down into a cold, dark void. She clung to the phone receiver as if it was all that kept her afloat.

Chapter Ten

Joe punched in the number of another old rodeo friend. He'd been calling everyone he could think of to start a search for Cody. The reaction he'd received had been overwhelming. His forgotten friends had quickly volunteered to start a search, and Joe realized he'd turned his back on so many good people. They hadn't intruded on his self-imposed exile. They'd waited patiently for him to heal.

As he spoke in low tones into the phone, he watched Marty, stoic, strong and pale as a winter moon. She paced back and forth, wearing a trail in her den carpet. With his tail tucked between his legs, Scout followed her, his nose bumping into the back of her calf periodically.

The police had arrived an hour earlier, questioned Flint, then Marty and finally Joe. The first thing they had to figure out was if someone had taken Cody. Or if he'd wandered off on his own. Marty didn't believe he'd do such a thing.

"Cody knows better than that," she'd told the steely-eyed detective.

Joe had his doubts. Cody was a mixed-up little six-year-old, with a neglectful father, an overprotective mother, and a dream for a real, tangible stick-together family. He'd had a rough few weeks, complicated by Joe's presence in his life.

In a short period of time, he'd turned the boy's world upside down by first stepping into his life, then by stepping out again. Guilt tumbled over Joe's heart like a rockslide, pummeling him for not committing to Marty, to her son, to a future.

What if something happened to Cody now?

Could he ever forgive himself? Could Marty?

Desperation and hot, boiling anger made his hands clench into fists. Why? Why had this happened? Why now, when things between Marty and him were falling into place?

As he dialed another number, fury burned inside him, choking him, paralyzing him. Once again, he was helpless. Helpless to do anything to find Cody, to help Marty. And impotence bred fear. It gnawed at him, biting through his steel-edged nerves.

"I don't know," Flint said from across the room. Exasperation made his voice boom. Shoving his hands through his blond hair, he collapsed into the leather chair as the detective jotted down notes in a tiny spiral notebook. "How was I supposed to know what to do? I thought he'd be safe in the truck for two lousy seconds. Hell, I took him to the bathroom at McDonald's. I knew not to let him go by himself. Marty always warned me about that." He gave the cop a confidential let's-be-buddies expression. "You never know what kind of weirdos are lurking around these days."

Joe heard a shuddered breath from Marty. He glanced at her, saw the tremor in her hand as her fingers pressed against her mouth, the tears swell in her eyes. Damn Flint

Thomas. Couldn't the jerk see how his tirade was affecting
Marty? Weren't things bad enough without his commen-
tary on the dark side of society?

A deep ache throbbed in Joe's chest for Marty…for
Cody. God, he knew the hopelessness, the fear, the futility.
He'd felt all the same emotions as he'd watched his wife
lie in a coma. At least, even knowing she wouldn't make
it, he was able to touch her hand, kiss her one last time,
be with her till the end.

But Marty couldn't hold Cody. Neither could he. Would
he always remember tucking the little boy into bed, drop-
ping a kiss on his brow and ruffling his hair as the last
time he'd seen him? What had he said to Cody last? Just
"G'night"? "See ya, kid"? What, dammit, what had he
said? He couldn't remember. He couldn't live with that.
He wished he'd had a chance to say he loved him….his
mother. Now it might all be too damn late.

He imagined Cody wet and cold, huddling in a dark
place and crying for his momma…his daddy. For the first
time he figured Cody would mean him. Joe. Not Flint. The
thought drove a well-honed, two-edged sword through his
heart. His chest burned, and his throat contracted with the
effort to contain his emotions.

He rubbed his eyes, feeling the grit beneath his lids, and
pinched the bridge of his nose. Glancing at Marty, he stood
and stretched his aching muscles. She looked so alone, so
confused, so tired. Dark smudges circled her eyes, making
them seem remote, as if she saw but didn't really comprehend all that was going on around her. A surge of love
welled within him. He wanted to protect her, shield her
from her fears, from life.

He went to her then and slipped an arm around her
shoulders. She seemed even smaller, as if she'd shrunk
inside her skin. But the second he touched her, she re-

coiled. Lifting her chin a notch, she squared her shoulders and shrugged off his supportive arm.

"It's okay," he said in a calm, soothing tone, and wondered if he'd startled her.

"Okay?" she shrieked. Her eyes became wild, like a caged animal's, as she turned on him. "No—" her lips compressed "—it's *not* okay. My son is missing. It'll never be okay until he's back home...here...where he belongs."

The muffled conversation in the room stopped. A squawk from a police radio added to the bleak silence that fell around them. All eyes turned to stare. Scout began to whimper, a high-pitched, forlorn whine.

"Marty." Joe dropped his hand to his side. He remained still, not backing away, not crowding her, either. His gut contracted with a sharp, slicing pain.

Her features contorted. Her hands clasped her stomach. "I'm sorry, Joe. I didn't mean—"

"It's—" He stopped himself from saying it was okay. She was right. It wasn't. It might never be again. "What can I do?"

She looked at him then, her eyes imploring, resting her last hope on him. A single tear slipped down her cheek. "Find my son." Her voice cracked. "That's all anybody can do."

With a quick nod, he made a decision. It might not have been his best or smartest. But it might be their only chance. This strong woman and her son had come to mean everything to him. He had to help them. He had to do *something*.

Because standing here, doing nothing, was going to drive him over the brink. And he knew Marty wasn't too far behind. He took her hand and stalked to the front door.

"Where are we going?" she demanded, dragging her feet, pulling against his grip.

"To find your son."

He stood her by the front door, bracketed her shoulders with his hands and peered deeply into her dark, cloudy eyes. He felt her tremble. "Stay here. I'll be right back."

Backtracking, he confronted the detective who'd been distracted by Marty's outburst from studying his notes and making phone calls in the kitchen. "She's all right. I know..." Joe said, his voice calm and firm, "I know you want us to stay here. But we know Cody. Better than anybody else. We'll do more good out there. Looking." His voice dropped to an urgent whisper. "She needs to get out and do something productive."

So do I! his mind screamed.

"That wouldn't be wise."

"We're not doing anything worthwhile here," Joe stated. "We've answered all your questions. She doesn't need to listen to her ex babble like an idiot about weirdos in the world. There's time to face that horror later. If that's what happened. But not now." *Not ever,* he pleaded silently with God. "Let's work together to find Cody."

The detective gave a brisk nod. His gaze shifted to her ex-husband then back to Joe. "Ms. Thomas is lucky to have you."

"We'll see about that." He gave a grim nod to the detective. "We'll be back in an hour, maybe less, I hope."

The detective handed him a cellular phone. "Take this. I'll call if we find out anything. Use it if you stumble on something. But don't, for God's sake, destroy any evidence. Don't be a goddamn hero. If you learn something call."

The cold hand of fear gripped Joe's stomach. What the hell were they going to find out there? He didn't know but he had to look, no matter what they found. Turning he clasped Marty's hand, needing to feel her close as a million terrifying possibilities as sinister as any police lineup filed through his mind.

Grabbing their coats as they stumbled out into the cold night. He loaded her in the truck and took off. For where, he wasn't exactly sure.

The minutes bled one into the another, and with each passing second hope drained out of Marty.

"What are we doing?" she said more to herself than to Joe, who drove slowly up and down street after street, his gaze shifting from the road to shadowed corners, searching...searching.... For what?

Would Cody be standing on a street corner? Was he hurt? Bleeding? She felt her nerves crumbling, her courage failing. What if... What if...what if.... Fear washed over her like a cold, hard rain, pelting her with guilt, flooding her with remorse. What if she'd stayed home? At least, a search could have been started earlier. What if she'd insisted on going with Flint and Cody? Then her son would probably be safely tucked into bed. Instead of out here in the cold, harsh real world.

"What do you mean?" Joe asked, his tone gruff, hard. "We're looking for your son." He glanced at her. She recognized that concerned look, as if he was checking to see if she'd gone crazy.

Maybe she had.

She sagged back against the cushioned seat. Her head pounded, her eyes burned from the strain. She shook her head back and forth and felt the tears she'd held off for the past couple of hours creep back up her throat again. "We're not going to find him."

"What kind of talk is that?"

"It's my fault...all my fault." A heavy cloud descended on her, blurring the image of Cody that she held in her mind. She pressed the heels of her hands hard against her eyes, punishing herself with the painful pressure. "I shouldn't have made Cody go with Flint. I should have stayed home. I should have—"

"There's a lot of things we *should* have done," Joe said. "But that's not always possible. You can't blame yourself."

"Who else is there to blame?" She glared at him. How dare he tell her not to do what he'd been doing to himself for five years! Any parent would feel responsible. As he did for his wife and child.

"Flint," Joe answered quietly.

She shrugged her shoulders. Okay, maybe there was one parent who'd have a hard time blaming himself. "There's always Flint. But for some reason I can't blame him. I want to. God, I want to. But I've always known he wasn't responsible." She pounded her fisted hand against the door. "I know that.

"So, it's me." She pressed her hand against her chest. "Don't you see? *I* should have known. I should have done something. Prevented this...somehow."

"How?" he asked, braking to a jarring stop alongside the road. A single street lamp illuminated a circle on the pavement, the dim light stealing the shadows from Joe's burning eyes. He gripped her shoulders hard and turned her to face him, giving her a gentle shake. "How could you have prevented this? Tell me."

"By *not* going with you."

"Wrong. Don't you see?" He leaned close to her, his face only inches from hers. "It's *not* your fault. Stop blaming yourself."

"You're one to talk, Joe Rawlins."

As if she'd slapped him, he jerked back. A wounded glint shot through his blue eyes. "What do you mean?"

"You blame yourself for your wife's death. For Sam's death. So why shouldn't I blame myself?"

"Cody's not dead," he said, his lips pulled tight.

"We don't know that," she said. For the first time they'd spoken of a very real possibility. She should have fallen apart at that very moment. But she didn't. A calm washed over her. She knew in her heart Cody wasn't dead. Wouldn't she know it, if he was? Her child was alive.

Slowly, Joe nodded and swallowed hard.

"Were you there?" she asked. "When the wreck happened?"

He leaned back against the driver's door and crossed his arms over his chest. "No."

"Are you a doctor?" She aimed the question at him, trying to make him understand how she felt. "Do you know how to pull someone out of a coma?"

"No."

"Then how could you have saved her? How? Would being in the car have made it better? If you'd been driving? If you'd been hit by the other car? If you had died?" She let the questions hang in the silence of the cab. "No," she answered for him. He might not believe it, but she did. She believed in him. She believed he'd survived for a reason. "Then you would have died. Then...then—"

A ragged sob severed her voice. She choked on a wave of bitter tears. Then...she wouldn't have had him to lean on now. And she needed Joe. Now, more than ever.

He stared at her. His blood ran icy-cold. He tried to shake off her words, push them out of his head. But they came back over and over again, pounding against his mind, driving out his self-accusations. If he blamed himself, then wasn't Marty to blame for Cody's disappearance? No, he couldn't believe that. He knew she would give her life for her child. As he would have for his wife and child.

How many times had he prayed in the hospital over his wife's inert body for God to take him, kill him right there, if only to give Samantha and his child another chance at life? But God hadn't listened.

Or had He?

Did He have another plan? Another purpose in store for Joe? What? Had He simply wanted to torture a poor cowboy? No, Joe didn't believe that, either.

Then did he have to accept Marty's logic?

Suddenly, it hit him, as if a bronc had kicked the slats out of him. He'd *wanted* to blame himself. It gave him some control in an otherwise uncontrollable situation. He'd never liked being out of control. Maybe that's why he'd taken chance by the reins and ridden bulls and broncs. Had circumstances, some piece of fate, stolen his wife and child? And no matter what he'd done, whether he'd been driving or not, would the results still have been the same?

"You're right," he said several minutes later. He noticed the windshield had begun to cloud up. He turned on the defroster. "You're right, Marty." It was all he could say, all he knew. "Neither of us is to blame. For my wife and child's death. For Cody's disappearance."

He lifted her hand into his, felt the smooth texture of her skin against his, felt the limp, helplessness in her fingers. Bending, he kissed the inside of her palm and stroked her hand, soothing himself as well as her. "What's that bumper sticker say— Stuff Happens? Maybe that's true. Maybe stuff does happen. Maybe things are meant to be. No matter how painful. No matter how trying."

She cut her eyes toward him. The corner of her mouth pulled upward. She braided her fingers with his, tightened her grip and sat up straighter. "But I can't let something happen to Cody. I've got to find him. As long as there is breath left in me. We're not going to let this happen to us. To Cody. We're going to find him. We have to find him."

"We will." He squeezed her hand and met her gaze honestly, boldly.

"But where?" A slight waver wilted the strength in her voice.

He nodded at the windshield. "There's the gas station where Flint stopped earlier...where Cody disappeared."

A cop car sat at the corner. It looked empty, deserted. Two cops stood inside the glass booth, speaking with the employee. Joe parked the truck and went around to help Marty out. One of the patrolmen came outside, and as Marty walked around the well-lit area, Joe spoke with the man quietly.

"We're bringing in dogs," the cop said. "Thought they might pick up a scent. Maybe give us a clue...something to go on. But with the rain...it might be too late to pick up a trail."

Joe nodded. "Something needs to break soon."

He watched Marty wander around, going from pump to pump, not touching anything but noticing everything. She pulled her coat tighter around her, clasping the opening together with a fist. Glancing up at the price sign, she stopped walking. She turned and looked back down the road. Then toward the west. The hair at the back of Joe's neck stood on end. He started to move toward her.

"This is— Joe," she called, her voice lifting. "This is where Cody and I stopped the morning we drove out to your ranch."

His nerves stretched tight. "Did something happen then?"

She shook her head. "He was excited. About you teaching him how to ride." She turned on her heel. "I'm sure this is the place."

"There's not another station for a mile or two in any direction." He scratched his chin with his thumbnail. "Didn't Flint say Cody was talking about me? And your ex was pretty fed up with all of that. It could have rubbed Cody the wrong way."

"You're his hero," she stated, her gaze telling him she admired him, too.

It brought no surge of pride inside Joe. It wouldn't mean anything if he couldn't find Cody. Then, it would fade into a distant memory. He couldn't let that happen.

"Flint's always disappointing Cody," she said. "Not just because he doesn't show up, or cancels their plans. But after they spend time together, I have to comfort Cody for some careless thing his father might have said." She grimaced. "He's not the most sensitive dad.

"But you've shown him a man can be different." She placed a hand on his arm. "Kind, loving. You showed him what a dad should be. And maybe that started a chain of reactions in him. What if he got mad at Flint? What if Flint wasn't too sensitive to Cody's hero-worship of you? What if when Flint went inside to pay—"

"Cody decided to go home or—"

"Go find *you*. The man who has been a father to him."

Joe nodded as the yoke of responsibility closed tightly about his neck. "If he remembered this place wasn't far from my ranch then..." He turned back to the officer. "Sergeant? Do you have a searchlight in your car?"

A minute later they were on the road, headed for Joe's ranch. He wanted to floor it, push the speed limit and reach his place fast. But he knew that would be foolish. Cody could be anywhere. He could be lost. He could have taken the wrong road. He could be huddled in a pile of weeds along the roadside.

So they drove at a snail's pace, Joe leading and the police car following, shining the high-beam light along the stretch of tall grass and barbed-wire fences.

Marty clenched her hands in her lap, her nails digging into her palm. Her eyes strained as she peered out the window and searched the roadside for her son. A vibration started in her chest and echoed outward from her heart, as if her very soul called out for Cody, crying his name over and over, in the hope that he'd hear her, sense her near.

When they reached Joe's wrought-iron gate, her hope plummeted. Cody could never have made it this far. They should have found him along the way. Maybe they missed him. Maybe he'd gotten lost, taken the road south rather than west. Maybe they were only pinning their hope on a fantasy. What if someone had taken her child?

The truck cab seemed to cave in on her then, as did the walls in her heart. She tried to push against them with the knowledge that there were other roads they could search, other motives, other possibilities. But she felt her hope begin to die. And that frightened her. She couldn't stop believing they'd find Cody. She couldn't give up. Not yet. Not ever.

As they rolled toward the brick house in the distance, the truck rocked and heaved over the ruts in the gravel road, the chassis creaked and groaned, the springs beneath poking at her. But she felt nothing. A numbness enveloped her, coated her senses with what seemed like glue. She closed her eyes and tried to take a deep breath, but her throat contracted, her lungs burned. She bit at her trembling bottom lip and leaned her face into her hands.

Joe shifted into park but left the engine idling. A deafening silence roared in her ears, filling the space between them, to throb and pulsate with each frantic beat of her heart. She felt his hand touch her arm, slide up and grip her shoulder. His fingers massaged her neck.

"Look there," he said. The calm certainty of his voice made her heart completely stop.

She lifted her head and stared out the windshield. The headlights illuminated a tiny figure curled up on the bench in the shadows of the porch. A car door slammed behind her, jarring her into action. She fumbled with the truck's door handle, pushed it open and ran for the porch, her legs once sluggish, gaining strength with each stride.

As she reached the top step, she slowed and tiptoed

across the porch. Her eyes adjusted to the dim light, and she saw Cody, snuggled inside his coat, wearing only one glove, and curled in a fetal position on the wooden bench. She saw his little chest rise and fall with each peaceful breath. Restraining the urgent need to gather him into her arms, she knelt in front of him, her body trembling uncontrollably.

She sensed Joe and the cop approaching from behind, heard their steps on the weathered wooden planks. Without taking her eyes off her son, she watched tiny puffs of air escape his parted, chapped lips. His hair was mussed, dampened on the ends. Smothering a sob, she smoothed a lock of dark brown hair off his forehead.

His eyes fluttered open. "Momma?" His voice cracked.

"Cody!" She scooped him into her arms, gathering him close, wrapping her arms around his body and pulling him down into her lap. Deep sobs racked her body as she tried to hold them back. She didn't want to frighten her son. But tears of relief, cleansing tears, flowed down her cheeks. She breathed in his scent. He smelled of wood smoke, damp wool and rain. His cheek felt cold against hers. She tangled her fingers in the hair along his nape and held him as if she'd never let him go.

After a few minutes he squirmed. "I can't breathe, Momma."

She released her tight hold on him and a bubble of joy escaped her in a mixture of laughter and tears. Pressing her forehead against his, she gazed into his big brown eyes. "Where have you been?"

"Here." He pushed back from her. "Where's Joe?"

"Right here, cowboy." He knelt beside them and ruffled Cody's hair.

"You weren't here. I came to see you. But you weren't here."

She heard anguish in her son's voice. "Why did you want to see Joe?"

His little shoulders lifted in a shrug. "'Cause he listens to me."

Glancing in Joe's direction, she watched the sinewy muscles along his neck contract. "Sorry about that, pal. If I'd known you were coming, I'd have been waiting." He patted Cody on the back and blinked back a tear in his own eye. "I'll always be here for you."

"Promise?" Cody asked, reaching for him.

"Promise." Joe hugged them both, folding them into his strong arms.

"You've got to promise me something, Cody," Joe said, his voice thick and rough with emotion.

Her son nodded and waited for Joe to continue.

"No more runnin' off without telling your momma where you're going. Deal?"

"Deal." He gave them a cheek-splitting grin that made Marty's heart roll completely over.

Even after the police officers had left, they sat that way for a long time, holding each other, cradling Cody between their warm bodies, rocking back and forth in a slow rhythm that lulled Marty into a sense of comfort and security, like a lullaby.

An hour later she was home again and, after the police and Flint had left, her house quieted down. Marty leaned against Joe, who rested against the door frame of Cody's bedroom. She pressed her face against his chest and breathed in his warm, inviting scent that, to her, smelled of home. He held her close, one hand idly traveling the length of her spine, the other toying with her hair. Together, they watched her son, safe beneath his covers, the night-light giving off a faint glow of protection around his bed. The whispered sound of his breathing soothed her.

"I want to stand here all night," she said, her voice muffled by Joe's thick shoulder.

"Then I'll stand here with you."

"All night?" she asked, hope straining her nerves.

"Forever," he answered.

Her arms tightened around his waist. She knew he would, too. She knew he'd always be there for her...and Cody. Only Joe could offer her the strength she needed in weak moments, only he would make her life complete.

"I don't want there to ever be a question that we're a family," he said, his breath teasing her forehead.

Smiling into the darkness, she said, "How do you plan to do that?"

He tipped her face toward his. His gaze made her pulse leap. In his midnight-blue depths, she saw a deep longing that matched her own. "We're going to have to get married for real. No more pretending."

She swallowed, not quite believing her ears. She knew Joe had sworn off commitments and responsibility. But she knew he'd realized tonight that he hadn't been at fault in the death of his wife and child. They'd both learned a lot in the past few weeks about family, commitment, love.

She knew without a doubt she could trust this man to always be there for her and her son. She also knew she loved him. Loved him more than she'd ever thought possible. Loved him with her whole heart.

"For Cody?" she asked, her heart still not quite believing this man could love her as completely as she loved and needed him.

"Nope." His gaze bore into her, imprinting the truth of his words on her soul. "For us."

He smoothed his hand over her jawline and cupped the side of her neck with a tenderness that made her insides contract. "I love you, Marty Thomas. I love your strength. I love how you stand up to me. I love how soft you are in my arms.'' He kissed her gently, moving his lips over hers slowly, seductively. Smiling against her mouth, he said, ''I love the way you look in the mornings, all disheveled.''

''You haven't seen me in—''

''Yes, I have. I think that's when I first started to love you. That first morning....'' He shook his head. His gaze grew solemn. ''Will you marry me?''

''Will you make those yummy cinnamon biscuits?''

''Every morning for the rest of your life.''

''Then, yes.'' She couldn't hold back the smile or the tears.

''Do you know when I finally realized I loved you?'' he asked, his voice deep and husky.

Unable to speak, she shook her head.

''When you cried for me. Just me.'' He kissed away her tears, as he kissed away her fears, sorrow and regret. Finally he captured her mouth with his and promised her a lifetime of tomorrows. ''But I don't want you to cry anymore.''

''You can't promise what the future holds. And I can't promise I won't ever cry again.''

''I know that. I've learned that no one can change what fate has in store. But we have to embrace every moment we have together. I don't want to waste any more time. I can promise I'll always be there for you.''

''As I'll be there for you.''

''I just want you to love me.'' His voice cracked.

''Always.'' She captured his strong jaw between her hands and kissed him back, opening to him, heart and soul. She knew how easy that promise would be. ''I do love you, Joe Rawlins.''

''Are you my daddy now?'' Cody asked sleepily, his voice coming out of the darkness.

Joe smiled. ''Yes, I am, son. Yes, I am.''

The love behind his words warmed Marty like sunshine in the middle of winter. She knew Joe would be her son's father. And he'd be her husband. Permanently.

* * * * *

Silhouette Romance
celebrates the joys
of first love in
VIRGIN BRIDES

September 1998:
THE GUARDIAN'S BRIDE
by Laurie Paige (#1318)
A young heiress, desperately in love with her
older, wealthy guardian, dreams of wedding the
tender tycoon. But he has plans to marry
her off to another....

October 1998:
THE NINE-MONTH BRIDE
by Judy Christenberry (#1324)
A widowed rancher who wants an heir and a prim librarian
who wants a baby decide to marry for convenience—but will
motherhood make this man and wife rethink their
temporary vows?

November 1998:
A BRIDE TO HONOR by Arlene James (#1330)
A pretty party planner falls for a charming, honor-bound
millionaire who's being roped into a loveless marriage. When
the wedding day arrives, will *she* be his blushing bride?

December 1998:
A KISS, A KID AND A MISTLETOE BRIDE (#1336)
When a scandalous single dad returns home at
Christmas, he encounters the golden girl he'd fallen
for one magical night a lifetime before.

Available at your favorite retail outlet.

Silhouette®

Take 2 bestselling love stories FREE

Plus get a FREE surprise gift!

Special Limited-Time Offer

Mail to Silhouette Reader Service™

3010 Walden Avenue
P.O. Box 1867
Buffalo, N.Y. 14240-1867

YES! Please send me 2 free Silhouette Romance™ novels and my free surprise gift. Then send me 6 brand-new novels every month, which I will receive months before they appear in bookstores. Bill me at the low price of $2.90 each plus 25¢ delivery and applicable sales tax, if any.* That's the complete price, and a saving of over 10% off the cover prices—quite a bargain! I understand that accepting the books and gift places me under no obligation ever to buy any books. I can always return a shipment and cancel at any time. Even if I never buy another book from Silhouette, the 2 free books and the surprise gift are mine to keep forever.

215 SEN CH7S

Name	(PLEASE PRINT)
Address	Apt. No.
City	State · Zip

This offer is limited to one order per household and not valid to present Silhouette Romance™ subscribers. *Terms and prices are subject to change without notice. Sales tax applicable in N.Y.

USROM-98 ©1990 Harlequin Enterprises Limited

MEN at WORK

All work and no play?
Not these men!

October 1998
SOUND OF SUMMER by Annette Broadrick
Secret agent Adam Conroy's seductive gaze
could hypnotize a woman's heart. But it was
Selena Stanford's body that needed saving—
when she stumbled into the middle of an
espionage ring and forced Adam out of
hiding....

November 1998
GLASS HOUSES by Anne Stuart
Billionaire Michael Dubrovnik never lost a
negotiation—until Laura de Kelsey Winston
changed the boardroom rules. He might
acquire her business...but a kiss would cost
him his heart....

December 1998
FIT TO BE TIED by Joan Johnston
Matthew Benson had a way with words
and women—but he refused to be tied
down. Could Jennifer Smith get him to
retract his scathing review of her art by
trying another tactic: tying him *up*?

Available at your favorite retail outlet!

MEN AT WORK™

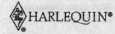 

Look us up on-line at: http://www.romance.net

PMAW3

For a limited time, Harlequin and Silhouette have an offer you just can't refuse.

In November and December 1998:

BUY **ANY** TWO HARLEQUIN
OR SILHOUETTE BOOKS and
SAVE $10.00
off future purchases

OR BUY ANY THREE HARLEQUIN OR SILHOUETTE BOOKS
AND **SAVE $20.00** OFF FUTURE PURCHASES!

(each coupon is good for $1.00 off the purchase of two
Harlequin or Silhouette books)

···

JUST BUY 2 HARLEQUIN OR SILHOUETTE BOOKS, SEND US YOUR
NAME, ADDRESS AND 2 PROOFS OF PURCHASE (CASH REGISTER
RECEIPTS) AND HARLEQUIN WILL SEND YOU A COUPON BOOKLET
WORTH **$10.00** OFF FUTURE PURCHASES OF HARLEQUIN OR
SILHOUETTE BOOKS IN 1999. SEND US 3 PROOFS OF PURCHASE AND
WE WILL SEND YOU 2 COUPON BOOKLETS WITH A TOTAL SAVING OF
$20.00. (ALLOW 4-6 WEEKS DELIVERY) OFFER EXPIRES
DECEMBER 31, 1998.

···

I accept your offer! Please send me a coupon booklet(s), to:

NAME: _____

ADDRESS: _____

CITY: _____ STATE/PROV.: _____ POSTAL/ZIP CODE: _____

Send your name and address, along with your cash register
receipts for proofs of purchase, to:

In the U.S.	In Canada
Harlequin Books	Harlequin Books
P.O. Box 9057	P.O. Box 622
Buffalo, NY	Fort Erie, Ontario
14269	L2A 5X3

PHQ4982

FOLLOW THAT BABY...

the fabulous cross-line series featuring the infamously wealthy Wentworth family...continues with:

THE SHERIFF AND THE IMPOSTOR BRIDE
by Elizabeth Bevarly
(Desire, 12/98)

When a Native American sheriff spies the runaway beauty in his small town, he soon realizes that his enchanting discovery is actually Sabrina Jensen's headstrong *identical* twin sister....

Available at your favorite retail outlet, only from

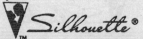

twins
on the doorstep

The Murdocks are back!
The adorable children from

STELLA BAGWELL'S
Twins on the Doorstep

series are all grown up and finding
loves of their own. You met Emily in
THE RANCHER'S BLESSED EVENT in
May 1998 and Charlie found love in
THE RANGER AND THE WIDOW WOMAN
in August 1998

Now it's Anna's turn!
Yes, the twins are about to discover true love
and Anna's the first to lose her heart in

THE COWBOY AND THE DEBUTANTE
(SR#1334, November 1998)

And in spring of 1999 look for Adam to find the woman
he can't live with—or without!

Only in Silhouette Romance.

THE MacGREGORS ARE BACK!

#1 *New York Times* bestselling author

NORA ROBERTS

Presents...

THE MacGREGORS:
Serena—Caine
December 1998

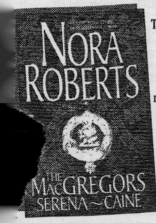

Two exciting stories from one exciting
author! Serena MacGregor doesn't
gamble on love, but irresistible
Justin Blade won't take no for an
answer! Attorney Caine MacGregor
meets his match in Diana Blade—and
must open his brooding heart to love.

Coming soon in
Silhouette Special Edition:

**March 1999: THE PERFECT
NEIGHBOR (SE#1232)**

Also, watch for the MacGregor
stories where it all began !

**February 1999: THE MacGREGORS: Alan—Grant
April 1999: THE MacGREGORS: Daniel—Ian**

Available at your favorite retail outlet, only from

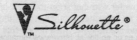

Silhouette ROMANCE™

COMING NEXT MONTH

#1336 A KISS, A KID AND A MISTLETOE BRIDE
—Lindsay Longford
Virgin Brides

They had shared one magical kiss, and it had seared Gabrielle O'Shea's soul forever. Now Joe Carpenter was back—with a six-year-old son in tow. Joe didn't believe he deserved Gabby in his life again, no matter how much he—and his son—wanted her. But some loves weren't meant to be denied....

#1337 BURKE'S CHRISTMAS SURPRISE—Sandra Steffen
Bachelor Gulch/Bundles of Joy

Burke Kincaid had returned to town with a mission—to win back his lost love, Miss Louetta Graham. And when Burke found out the lovely Louetta was on her way to the altar with another man, he vowed he'd do whatever it took to be the groom at the end of the aisle.

#1338 GUESS WHAT? WE'RE MARRIED!—Susan Meier
Texas Family Ties

There was something missing in her marriage, and it wasn't just Grace Wright's memory! Her husband, Nick, was hiding something. But though she couldn't remember her marriage, the emotions Nick stirred up in her weren't easily forgotten....

#1339 THE RICH GAL'S RENTED GROOM —Carolyn Zane
The Brubaker Brides

An instant family was needed—and fast! So Patsy Brubaker went out and rented herself one handsome husband and two adorable kids. But the more time Patsy spent with sexy Justin Lassiter and their two "children," the more she wanted to keep this borrowed family forever.

#1340 STRANDED WITH A TALL, DARK STRANGER
—Laura Anthony

She had never wanted a man to get close to her again. But then mysterious Keegan Winslow showed up at Wren Matthews' cabin during a blizzard. Trapped, Wren didn't want to fight her attraction to Keegan...but could she trust her heart to this handsome stranger?

#1341 A BABY IN HIS STOCKING—Hayley Gardner

One passionate encounter with her soon-to-be ex-husband, Jared, had left Shea Burroughs an expectant mother. And although Jared claimed he wasn't the crib and cradle type, Shea hoped that the season of miracles could transform Jared into a Santa Claus daddy.